You Will Never See Any God

 *Stories*

ERVIN D. KRAUSE

Edited and with an introduction by Timothy Schaffert

University of Nebraska Press | Lincoln and London

Publication of this volume was assisted by a grant from the
Friends of the University of Nebraska Press.

"The Right Hand" is reprinted from *Prairie Schooner* 33.1
(Spring 1959) by permission of the University of Nebraska
Press, copyright 1959 by the University of Nebraska Press.
"The Metal Sky" and "The Snake" are reprinted from *Prairie
Schooner* 35.2 (Summer 1961) by permission of the University
of Nebraska Press, copyright 1961 by the University of
Nebraska Press. "The Quick and the Dead" is reprinted from
Prairie Schooner 34.1 (Spring 1960) by permission of the Uni-
versity of Nebraska Press, copyright 1960 by the University of
Nebraska Press.

Library of Congress Cataloging-in-Publication Data
Krause, Ervin D.
[Short stories. Selections]
You will never see any God: stories / Ervin D. Krause; edited
and with an introduction by Timothy Schaffert.
pages   cm
ISBN 978-0-8032-4976-9 (paper : alk. paper)—
ISBN 978-0-8032-5407-7 (pdf)—ISBN 978-0-8032-5408-4 (ePub)
—ISBN 978-0-8032-5409-1 (mobi)
I. Schaffert, Timothy. II. Title.
PS3611.R3767 A6 2014   813'.6—dc23   2013041641

Set in Arno Pro by Laura Wellington.
Designed by J. Vadnais.

For Loretta

Contents

Acknowledgments

Over the years, Ervin Krause's family and friends remained fiercely committed to the author's memory and the work he left behind. We should all be so lucky to have such a devoted village of archivists. Most significant among them has been Loretta Krause, my dear friend and research partner. Loretta not only saved notebooks, drafts, and correspondence but has generously shared her memories of Ervin from their life together. I'm extremely grateful for Loretta's kindness, humor, and spirit.

I'm also grateful for the time and attention that Marlene and Hank Krause have given to the project and the archives they've maintained—material that dates back to Ervin's high school years. And it's been a great pleasure to learn more about Ervin through his close friend and colleague Richard Goodman.

Special thanks to Kristen Elias Rowley of the University of Nebraska Press for her shepherding of this project. Ted Kooser has provided key perspective on the period and Karl Shapiro's role in Ervin's work. And many thanks to Susan Belasco for her support and encouragement.

Thanks also to Kurt Andersen, David Manderscheid, Judy

Slater, Wendy Katz, Kay Walter, Leta Powell Drake, Amber Antholz, Hilda Raz, Owen King, and Rhonda Sherman. And special thanks to Rodney Rahl for his insights and his enthusiasm for all my various literary endeavors.

This collection celebrates the tradition of the small literary journal and its decades-long commitment to the short-story writer. Some of the stories in this collection first appeared in *Prairie Schooner* ("The Right Hand," "The Metal Sky," "The Quick and the Dead," "The Snake") and *Northwest Review* ("The Shooters," "The Witch"). The O. Henry Awards prize stories anthology reprinted "The Quick and the Dead" and "The Snake." Other of Krause's stories appeared in *University Review—Kansas City, Literary Review, New Letters,* and *College English.*

Introduction

In the stories of Ervin Krause, men and women are often unforgiving of each other's trespasses. But their fiercest grudges are with the land and the sky. The characters are troubled by floods and parched earth, battered by "vivid, hurting" snow and intense summer sun. Sometimes nature wins in these struggles and sometimes humans do, but in Krause's fiction it's never a fair fight, and it's often brutal.

In one of Krause's most heart-wrenching and terrifying passages, in "The Metal Sky," a farmer examines the intricate beauty and flight of a butterfly as he struggles to stay alive after an accident. Pinned, bleeding, beneath his own machinery, he seeks companionship in death while also envying the insect's light-as-air indifference:

> He brought his fingers up and then very carefully and quickly snapped the fingers shut on the arched yellow wings. The butterfly struggled, but its wings were caught and its fragile black body vibrated in its writhings. The yellow dust on the wings rubbed off and filtered down, lightly.

It will know I am not dead, the man thought. It alone, if nothing else, will know. He held the fragile wings of yellow light, with the wings so delicate he could not even feel them between his hardened hands. The butterfly tried to move and could not and the claws of its legs clasped the air.

Had Krause lived to write longer, to write more, we would almost certainly have come to have a sense of the *Krausian*—fiction characterized by the stark, haunting poetry of his language, the treachery of his landscapes, the moral and fatal failings of his unblessed characters. His stories are tantalizing portraits of sad hamlets surrounded by fields of failed crops and rising rivers, grim little worlds as gritty as the settings of pulp crime. These stories aren't so much about survival as they are about the characters' determination to outlive all the other hard-living men and women around them.

Though his stories are told without sentiment, with all of pulp's electric tension and lack of mercy, they nonetheless have the gentle but insistent rhythms of folktale. There's life, then there's death. These are tales that command retelling; they're cautionary, while inviting you to perversely delight in every character's every reckless act. The stories play on our memories of shadowy figures and childhood fears, the countryside peopled with witches and skinflints, the nights prowled by wolves and scrutinized by an "agonized and lamenting" moon. And above all, a legendary bad luck plagues the characters' minor lives.

"There was nothing dead that was ever beautiful," considers the farmer of "The Metal Sky" in a last stab at philosophizing, as he perishes beneath a fallen tractor, unfound, unnoticed, in a field to which he has dedicated his life.

Some of this country squalor Krause knew by heart, having grown up in poverty, among tenant farmers. The Krauses moved from plot to plot across Nebraska and Iowa in the years immediately following the Depression. Krause's fiction depicts lives and fates he strove to avoid. His characters pontificate in saloons, condemning the morals of others as they slowly get sloshed; his men and women have extramarital affairs in old cars on winter nights; they traffic in gossip, terrorize their neighbors; they steal, they hunt, they spy. A child's innocent curiosity can turn sinister in a minute—children see things too terrible too soon. These are stories of crimes big and small, with no law in sight.

While Krause's characters contended with all sorts of demons, both within and without, Krause himself grew up under the strong moral guidance of Lutheran parents. Krause was born in Arlington, Nebraska, on June 22, 1931, to German Russian immigrants and grew up with four brothers. When he was fifteen, "his father fell paralyzed from a stroke," writes Joseph Backus, a friend of Krause's and an early devotee of his fiction, "to linger six years unable to speak, only listening as Erv would sit and read to him. But great purpose and principle drove the boys' mother, who kept them in line with knuckle-thunks to the head or the tweak of an ear."

Old Moder, as the boys' mother was known, was not old at all. But stout and sturdy, her hair pulled back tight, she was an intimidating presence. She instilled in her young men a respect for education, but she seems also to have inspired a great sense of urgency—they studied hard, they went to college, they excelled in their professions. One son became an aeronautical engineer, one a professional baseball scout, one a doctor, one a farmer. Ervin proved both poetically and mechanically minded; a popular family legend has it that he was so expert in his high school science classes that the school never had to hire a substitute—

Krause readily stepped in to instruct whenever the teacher was out. While pursuing his bachelor's degree in physics and math at Iowa State University, he contributed fiction and poetry to the school's literary journal.

In between his bachelor's degree and graduate school, Krause worked as a technical writer for MacDonald Aircraft in St. Louis and served eighteen months in the Air Force, stationed in England. Krause entered the master's program in English at the University of Nebraska–Lincoln in 1956, the same year that poet Karl Shapiro took the reins of *Prairie Schooner*, the venerable literary quarterly that has been published by the English Department since its first issue in 1927.

Krause's relationship with *Prairie Schooner*, and Shapiro's mentorship, would rapidly advance Krause's writing career, but it would also toss him into the center of controversy when his story "Anniversary" was declared "obscene" by the university's dean of the College of Arts and Sciences—leading to an act of censorship that made national news.

As an editor, Shapiro showed a rigorous commitment to Krause's work; "Anniversary" was to be the seventh story by Krause to appear in *Prairie Schooner*. The first, "Daphne," was published in 1958. "The Quick and the Dead," published in *Prairie Schooner* in 1960, was reprinted in *Prize Stories 1961: The O. Henry Awards*, along with stories by Tillie Olsen, Reynolds Price, Arthur Miller, Peter Taylor, and John Updike. In 1961 Shapiro promoted Krause's work in a bold move: he featured three of Krause's stories in the summer issue and boasted of it on the front cover with the same typographic fanfare he had previously allowed Walt Whitman and Henry Miller.

One of the three stories was "The Snake," which went on to

become widely reprinted over the next several years and earned Krause another appearance in the O. Henry Awards anthology (alongside fiction by Terry Southern, Jessamyn West, Joyce Carol Oates, and Ellen Douglas). Textbook editors have proven particularly partial to "The Snake"—the story, with its brevity and efficiency and its powerful examination of cruelty and punishment, lends itself well to instruction in craft and analysis. Metaphor, motif, theme, allusion, conflict, foreshadowing, imagery—students of writing and literature can take the back off the clock and see how the cogs all click together. What lends the story its authority, however, is a bit more difficult to define. At the heart of it is a small act of passion on an ordinary morning of routine farm work, one that will likely change the relationship between the two characters—a boy and his uncle—for the rest of their lives.

By the time Krause's story "Anniversary" was accepted for a 1963 edition of *Prairie Schooner*, Krause had moved to Honolulu, having taking a teaching job at the University of Hawaii. He was now married—at the University of Nebraska he had met Loretta Loose, who had spent a fast-paced year in a new master's program in theater, performing role after role in the campus playhouse. Ervin and Loretta were young artists in love; they were married in 1961.

In Hawaii Krause taught creative writing and continued to write fiction and poetry—but his characters remained, determinedly, in the Midwest. According to Loretta, Ervin recognized the importance of place to a young writer seeking to establish an original voice. He knew the land and the life of the Midwest too well to ever finish with it, and he knew that such knowledge gave his work a necessary edge of authenticity. His notebooks—currently housed with his papers in the archives of the University of Nebraska–Lincoln's Love Library—are riddled with sketches of characters and places, many drawn from his childhood on the plains.

The censored story, "Anniversary," is one of only a few of Krause's stories to be set in an actual city—and it's this specificity that might have provoked the anxiety of university administrators. In "Anniversary" a character named McDonald returns to Lincoln, Nebraska, over holiday break to visit Wanda, a woman with whom he'd had an affair during his master's program in an unnamed English department. McDonald, now an assistant professor of English at the University of Missouri, is a bit of a prig in the making. He's a womanizer (the narrator provides insight into his sexism when the story describes the "birdy" female graduate students McDonald dated as having "unsexed bodies like store-window dummies and faces like parakeet beaks"), generally insensitive (the "fairies" in the department, we're told, had approached McDonald "in sly, nuzzling, knee-touching familiarity"), and largely misanthropic (in a single sentence businessmen are "bland-faced" and sergeants are "gross-faced"). But he's lonely, and desperately so, and "Anniversary" is easily Krause's most chilling story.

McDonald's emptiness contrasted with Wanda's sweet nature and vulnerability further demonstrates an exploration of cruelty and frailty that so motivated Krause—most notably in his story "The Snake." McDonald is even a writer himself and publishes his work in literary journals.

"Why do you write about such dark and unhappy things?" Wanda asks. "You should take things more lightly."

Ultimately, McDonald convinces himself that Wanda is as dead inside as he is, and after lovemaking he confronts her with a sociopath's disgust. All along, Krause articulates McDonald's mean spirit in dark prose worthy of Richard Yates.

The prose proved too dark for university administrators, or the sex was described too explicitly. It's unclear what most offended. Different stories abound regarding the true impulse to censor and how the story came to cross the desk of a dean not typically involved in *Prairie Schooner*'s editorial processes. But Dr. Walter Millitzer, dean of the university's College of Arts and Sciences at the time, took official responsibility. Millitzer removed the story from galleys without Karl Shapiro's knowledge. Shapiro then publicized his immediate resignation from his editorship of *Prairie Schooner* and his intention to leave the university. He also read "Anniversary" on a local radio station. "Anniversary," however, has never been published until now.

In an article in the *New York Times* dated May 24, 1963, Millitzer is quoted as describing the story as "obscene and in poor taste." Shapiro, in the same article, defends the story as simply one of "washed out love with a couple of bedroom scenes." The headline of the article indicated Shapiro's response to the controversy: "Shapiro Quits Nebraska U.; Cites 'Editorial Tampering.'"

Krause wrote to Clifford Hardin, the university's chancellor, from Hawaii a few days after the censorship of his short story made the *New York Times* and other newspapers across the country: "The university must stand with fierce pride and integrity against the forces of ignorance and prejudice and stupidity; the university must defend the right of the artist to speak. You have denied what a university must stand for."

Krause courted controversy, addressing subjects such as infidelity, abortion, racism, homosexuality, abuse. The "censorship," as he came to refer to it, didn't change his direction or slow him down. He even wrote a novel—never published—about the English department and the *Prairie Schooner* incident, titled "The Censoring." But the removal of "Anniversary" from *Prairie Schooner*, and the dean's dismissal of the story, deeply troubled him. When he received a letter from Bernice Slote, Shapiro's successor as editor of *Prairie Schooner*, letting him know she wouldn't be publishing "Anniversary" but that "we are strong for you, and hope to continue promoting your work," Krause fired back. "In case your exquisite sensibility does not fully grasp the import," he wrote, "you will never get another story from me, at any time, under any conditions, until the true situation regarding the *Schooner* is clarified and exposed."

But a far more devastating development than the censorship awaited Krause; a year after the dean's public denouncement of "Anniversary," Krause was diagnosed with Hodgkin's disease. For his last seven years—he died on Thanksgiving Day in 1970, at the age of thirty-nine, in the house in Hawaii in which Loretta still lives—he researched experimental cancer treatment, managed his academic career, and wrote new fiction and poetry. Though he never abandoned the pursuit of a book deal, he now wrote with a mind toward a literary legacy that he knew might come only after his death. He often spoke to Loretta of his delight in imagining college sophomores attempting to decipher his meanings.

With "The Snake," a story still assigned in the classroom, he got his wish of inspiring such careful analysis of his work—"The Metal Sky" and "The Quick and the Dead" have also been reprinted in textbooks and anthologies. But the publication of a collection of his stories proved challenging. Compiled together, the stories were too dark, he was told in rejection letters. And as Loretta sought upon his death to fulfill her husband's dream of publishing a book, the work's rough and unflinching vision continued to prove too despairing for both commercial and literary publishing.

In a symposium held at the Library of Congress in 1965, Karl Shapiro, still stinging from the censorship controversy, spoke of the role of a journal in defining literature: "A work printed in the literary magazine has only two destinations: the book or oblivion." When pressed on this issue by his fellow panelists ("Surely it's damn good for a writer to be published and to be read by serious readers and serious writers whether or not his particular work is going to be put into hard cover," huffed Jules Chametzky, then editor of the *Massachusetts Review*), Shapiro did "stand corrected." He went on to say, "I have come back to the old-fashioned, possibly reactionary point of view, that the function of the little magazine is greater today than ever before; more than ever it has to resist the bait of joining society."

Krause certainly resisted that bait, writing as he did about characters who themselves chafed at the notion of social engagement. His short stories were respected and rewarded in his lifetime when published individually in journals, and he was well established as a short-story writer by the early 1960s. Not only did he receive recognition from the O. Henry Prize but also from the *Best American Short Stories* series, as edited by Martha Foley and David Burnett, in which his stories were cited as among the year's most distinctive in 1961 ("The Quick and the Dead"), 1962 ("The Snake," "The Metal Sky," "The Fall"), and 1967 ("The Witch," "The Shooters"). But without a collection, his stories were destined to be lost. "And while the magazine itself is expendable," Shapiro continued in his Library of Congress presentation, "the book, no matter how bad, is not. It is practically impossible to lose or destroy a book; the Library knows this only too well."

Though Shapiro might have overstated the unlikelihood of a book's expendability (even Shapiro's own acclaimed, award-winning collections of poetry are currently in a state of neglect), the literary hierarchy of the twentieth century was shaped and ordered according to the prominence of an author's books among readers, publishers, and scholars. And in losing Ervin Krause's voice, we lost a graphic and captivating representation of post-Depression farm life.

With this collection, Krause's stories—no longer confined to the archives of middle-twentieth-century literary journals—can enter a new level of consideration. The stories included here are only a fraction of Krause's complete body of work; some of his stories exist only in handwritten form in his many spiral-bound notebooks. ("Old Schwier," a story included in this collection, a folktale about maniacal power and devastating regret, is one that Krause never typed nor submitted to journals.)

The stories Krause tells are bleak but they're exciting in their raw poetic vigor, and they're vital to our understanding of these rural men and women and their paradoxical nature of a complicated simplicity. These are the larger-than-life legends of a small locality, stories of personal defeat and ruination that most often went untold in a God-fearing community. While gossip and suspicion rend apart these characters' lives, the narrative is driven by the reader's very same desire to learn of the intimate transgressions of the sinners and the sinned against.

"Mythic," Richard Poirier said of Krause's story "The Snake," which he selected for *Prize Stories 1963: The O. Henry Awards.* In his introduction to the anthology (which awarded "The Snake" second place; first prize went to Flannery O'Connor's classic "Everything That Rises Must Converge"), Poirier writes, "[Krause] is a writer with great meditative dignity of address. . . . [His images and symbols] are necessarily the most obvious he could borrow from literature and the Bible. He is not in the least complacent about this symbolism, however, making of its contemporary relevance more a mystery than an assumption and showing how it comes into being within the blood stream of people who are not aware of the Biblical analogies for what they are doing."

YOU WILL NEVER SEE ANY GOD

Spring Flood

On a hot Thursday afternoon in late May the rain began to fall, warmly at first, spreading gently over the Iowa farmland like warm congealed humidity. The chillness came the next day with the darkening clouds, and the lightning strokes had the cold malevolence of snakes' tongues. The sullen gullies and the little creeks filled and raged, and the black water sluiced into the placid river, the river itself altering, becoming plugged with dirt and carcasses, a black mucus. Animals floated dead on the roiling water, a sheep or a calf twisted, bloated and huge, and drawn down again, ghost-like, into the black. Muskrats, like pockets of furry mud, paddled without panic, reaching for the banks. Perceptibly the river rose.

Already by Friday evening, or what the people along that river thought to be evening in the somber gloom of rain, the banks of the river were at last overlapped and the levees topped, and the water pulsed through the breaks suddenly with quick and ugly movement like that of an angry reptile's head. After that first rush of water there was the steady ooze upward, seeping across the rich bottom land, isolating farmyards and drowning the new crops in the lowlands, and the flooded river began to back water up the little, rain-heavy creeks.

The water carried with it fallen trees and the muck of a thousand Iowa farms, the litter of cornstalks and dry hemp and tumbleweeds, driving startled living things ahead, a bedraggled deer or two, the squawking birds, the rabbits, scarred turtles, water rats, and fish too, mud-colored ancient gar and carp, transported by the flood surge beyond the levees into the dead and quiet fields of three-foot-deep water on the lowlands. The rain fell and the water rose and the farmers slogged through the mud of farmyards, sullenly, and fed the wilting cattle and retreated again to huddle in their raincoats beneath eaves.

"She never stop pouring," old Gerber said to young Dahlman. Gerber lived in a shack along the river. The shack was submerged already and he had taken refuge in Dahlman's corncrib, where Dahlman always had to put him up whenever Gerber needed it. The need was usually once a year, when the rains came in the spring and the river came up, and then Gerber appeared at his place in the corncrib, stinking and mudded over like some grizzled river reptile, saying the water was up again.

Gerber was a legacy from the time of grandfather Dahlman; he was immensely old, no one knew how old for sure, and Gerber himself never said. He had once been a hired hand for the grandfather, and a worthless one, old Dahlman had always said, and he had built a shack on the Dahlman land by the river and there he stayed, holed up in the mud and the mosquito slime and remaining alive through two generations of Dahlmans and aging not at all. For as long as young Dahlman could remember, old Gerber came to the Dahlman house once a day for the noon meal, which the woman was forced to feed him. When the father died they tried to ignore him, but Gerber rattled the screen door and said the old man and the old old man before him had fed him and that they would too. Young Dahlman said he would not, and he held the door against the old man and said, "Go away Gerber, we don't want you; go away, you hear, don't come back." The old man stood there gripping the screen door sill with his turtle-claw hands, panting like a hungry dog, his eyes tiny and evil and undeniable, and he sat upon the wicker chair on the porch, panting and moaning half through the afternoon until at last the exasperated wife scooped up a pie tin full of potatoes and stew and shoved it out the door to him. He ate and left and reappeared the next noon. So he won, and they fed him the one meal although he did nothing at all, never had, for them or for anyone else. The other two meals a day, if he ate them, he got himself. The supplies he needed he stole, oats from Dahlman's bins, corn from Dahlman's fields, and occasionally, with resignation as much as anything else, Dahlman provided Gerber with a sack of flour or sugar and a can of coffee. Whatever else Gerber got he speared from the river. He had three spears, ancient things, with smoothworn handles, and Gerber used them with skill. He could stalk fish as no man could, and he could hit the sluggish carp with expertness and surprising quickness and fierceness when he did choose to strike. He ate carp and some people said he even ate gar, those bullet-shaped prehistoric scavengers that thrived on the sewage of the rivers, but no one had seen enough of Gerber to know for sure what he survived on. Dahlman had invaded the tarpaper shack a few times and had looked in the black pot on the stove at the simmered chunks like live things within, and he could never tell what was live or dead, what newly entered or weeks there, what eaten or uneaten.

So Gerber lived in the ancient, mudded shack, a creature of mud himself, like something that had arisen one time out of a swamp and proved to be alive. He was without forebears and without offspring, this legacy of two generations past who appeared like a wart and subsisted like one, tough, implacable, ineradicable, with no connection to anything living or dead.

He hunched over and shook himself like a wet dog and said, "Sure some rain."

Dahlman nodded and said nothing. He watched the heavy sky and the water spilling whitely from the roofs.

"This river she come up higher than you remember," Gerber said. "She bring fish."

"And muck and trees and god knows what else," Dahlman said.

"Ya, trees come across the road. Trees in your bottom field."

And Dahlman knew he meant floating dead trees had washed in over the levees, to lie with the rest of the flood muck in the fields.

"Not big trees," Gerber said with a tiny gesture of his knotted dark hand. The hand disappeared within his sleeve again like the black foot of a turtle withdrawing into its shell.

"Animals come out too," Gerber went on, his voice removed and hollow. "I see lot of rabbits and coons come out of their holes to high ground. Some drown."

"The land drowns too in this flood. That is the trouble," Dahlman said.

"I see muskrat, but the fur is no good, otherwise I kill them. Muskrats almost drowned from swimming. And one snake, black and all muddy, riding on top of a tree that float by."

"A snake?"

"Ya, the tree float by down there," pointing towards the river or where the river usually flowed, "and the snake there mad and wet, holding on." There was a faint wheezing, and Dahlman listened and wondered if old Gerber actually laughed, and he turned to look and saw the old toothless mouth, crimped at the edges and black from mud and tobacco and the motion of the mouth like a turtle's beak. "That snake mad as hell, not liking the water much, holding on."

"No. Most snakes don't like water. Nothing likes it in flood time."

"It was a mad old snake, not a big one, so long . . ."—measuring out eighteen inches between his black turtle hoof hands—"It look up at me as the tree float by. I spit at it." Again the faint wheezing sound. Dahlman shuddered, from the rain, from the thought of the wet and angry snake riding a tree into his field, from the old man beside him, from his helpless disappointment with everything that spring.

The wife called for dinner and they went up through the pouring chill rain to the house. Dahlman took off his overshoes and he looked down across the little slope to beyond the barn where the water was dim through the rain. The water had seeped to within one hundred yards of the barn and it spread over the flat land all the way to the river. There was a floating edge of scum, ragged like teeth, all along the cornstalk-littered field, and down there in the water a pair of tree trunks floated dimly and listlessly, like hulks of hippopotamus, only the bulk of trunk showing, and the spiny branches broken or hidden in the rain-mist.

"Water never reach the farmyard," Gerber said. "It have to come up twenty feet more before it reach here."

Dahlman shook his head at this reassurance, knowing that old Gerber had never worked the land, had given no time to the soil, did not even comprehend the land swallowed by that flood. Dahlman turned abruptly to the door. "Bernice," he said, "is Gerber's plate ready?"

The woman said nothing, only brought the pie tin full of food out and set it on the washing machine on the porch without looking at either of them, and she went in again. Gerber sat down on the old wooden chair and began to eat with his fingers, ignoring the fork Dahlman's wife always set out. He wheezed to himself and gummed at the food with energy and offered some to the dog, but the dog, still distrustful of Gerber after all the eight years of its life, lifted his rain-wet body and backed away to a distant corner of the porch.

The old black gums exposed as Gerber grinned at the dog. "Old Gerber gonna eat fish pretty soon. Lot of carp in that field out there; gonna get my spear and get some carp. You be glad to eat from my hand then, old dog. I feed you carp guts, you eat."

"Dirty old man," the wife said when Dahlman went in and closed the door.

"I know, I know," Dahlman said wearily. Impatiently he swung about the room talking loudly, knowing that Gerber could hear if he wanted to listen. "Why doesn't he go somewhere else, to some neighbor's place maybe? Why does he have to come here? He eats our food and drinks our water, and he prowls around stealing our corn and chickens, and making himself a damned nuisance. I wish the old devil would die."

"Oh Ronald," she said in mild, unspirited rebuke.

"Well why not?" he said. "I wish he would. Just because the old man fed him and gave him a place to sleep, he thinks he's part of us now. He has a hold on this place. There's nothing we can do, not until he's dead and gone."

"But to wish that," the wife said, shaking her head. "At least you shouldn't say it."

"Oh, it's right all right. Gerber should die. He's dirty and foul, foul breath, foul smell, foul mouth, everything. He should die. Damn him."

"Ronald," she cried. "You get so upset when you start with him. I wish you wouldn't."

"I wish I wouldn't, too. I'd like to be free of that for once. I would like some time to live for just a little while knowing that he's not there skulking around like some damned mangy dog. I would like to be free of him."

"He can hear you out there," she murmured.

"I don't care."

"I'm afraid of him, sometimes. I don't know what he might do if he got angry at us."

Dahlman threw up his hands and went off into the next room to stare out the window at the rain and the gray-sludge lake formed beyond the cattle barns. The gloom lowered over the land and the sky bled. He could not see beyond the water in the cornstalk field.

"Damn this rain," he muttered, but loud enough for his wife to hear. "The crops are gone, ruined, and even the oats and soybeans on the hills will be finished if it rains any more. And that old bastard sits out on our porch and eats our food. Do you know what he said to me?"

"What?" she asked.

"He's happy that there's a flood, because he can spear carp. Now he can eat carp!"

"It can't last much longer," she said. "It just can't."

"Maybe he'll go out there, spearing fish, and he'll drown. Maybe his shack will wash away." (And if Gerber lived, he would have me help him build a new shack, Dahlman added to himself.) He looked out the west window towards where Gerber's hovel usually crouched like a beaten, bedraggled dog, but the rain hid that too. "Maybe he will drown and the shack will go, and we'll see nothing of Gerber again."

"He's part river gar now," the wife said. "He will never drown."

Dahlman's face grew gloomy with the thought and the rain. Outside he saw Gerber detach himself from the mudded concrete porch steps where he had eaten and move formless and black and slow across the yard, leaving great clumps of prints as he walked. At the middle of the yard Gerber turned and looked up to the house, and his face, aged and gray-yellow, mal-colored, lifted and the old eyes fell upon Dahlman, and Dahlman jerked back from the window as if he should not be there watching, and he forced himself to the window again. The ancient man in the yard dug within the bib of his overalls with their slippery black sheen, extracted a pinch or two of tobacco, hooked the tobacco and his black fingers behind his yellow lips, and the hand came away. All the while he looked at the house. And then his mouth opened a little, perhaps in a smile, perhaps to chew the tobacco, perhaps to urge the dog which stood dripping and forlorn in the middle of the yard, the dog afraid of him and hating him, yet going wherever Gerber went, to squat on his trembling, frightened haunches ten feet away and look at the foul old man who spat at him. Gerber turned and went on, creating again the ponderous prints in the yard mud, and the wet dog trailed after, delicately lifting his feet, searching his way, but the dog too growing muddy. Gerber disappeared within the corncrib. Dahlman, watching, knew what he did, knew he found his corner among the dirty empty sacks, pulled the sacks over his legs and chewed his tobacco and inhaled the dust and watched the squatting dog.

"He said he saw a snake out there on a tree," Dahlman said softly, half to himself.

"A snake," she said, startled, pausing in her motion in the kitchen.

"The tree was floating, he said, and the snake was on the tree."

"Oh I don't like that," she said.

"It's nothing," he said.

"But to see a snake now, with all this rain . . ."

"What? You're not superstitious, are you, Bernice? One little snake is the least of our worries."

"But we've never had snakes around this place."

"It's nothing," he repeated. "Gerber probably made it up, knowing it would frighten you." He stroked his forehead. "If the rain would only stop. Then Gerber would go back to his shack; that would be better at least."

"I hope snakes don't come up on the yard is all," she was saying.

"Might help clean out the mice if they did. Anyway, there's only one and he's stuck out there somewhere, out in this goddamn rain."

"Don't get upset again, Ronald," she said, coming to him, touching him with her hand dried on her apron. "Come eat dinner, Ronald. Gerber is gone; we can eat now."

The rain fell yet two more days out of the ragged scuds of cloud that were like black cotton clumps ripped from their box. On the fifth day after it began, the rain slowed to a warm drizzle and the drizzle was patched with rising mist, and finally broken clouds let the sun through and the heat was intense suddenly where the sun was. The heat fell upon the land, sending up clouds of mist from the submerged flat lands of the river bottom. The water receded a little, leaving lines of cornstalk trash, foamed white lines like circles on bathtubs, ugly and vermin-ridden. In the fields the flood-driven branches of trees subsided in mud and the one true tree trunk settled in hip-deep water in the middle of Ronald Dahlman's field.

When the farm lanes had dried a little, after two days of the muggy sunshine, Dahlman took the tractor out to survey the fields. He could not go far, for the water still rode high to the tractor axles down towards the river. He came back to the house, cursing.

"The levees will have to be dynamited to get the water out," he told his wife. "I'll have to spend the fall rebuilding them." He swore. His wife clucked in commiseration. "And I can't even make a break in the levee until the river is down again."

And so he waited with rabid impatience. He put on his six-buckle overshoes and strode about the muddy yards like one trapped, from the barn to the hog house, and out to the water's edge fifty yards beyond that to look at the rotted tooth-edge of cornstalk litter there in the field, and back again he stormed, sweating in the magnified wet heat of the scalding sun.

But Gerber was pleased. The pipe-black face was lit with an anticipation, the eyes mere pinpoints of pupils in the leather tortoise folds that were his eyelids, were happy, and the toothless, lipless black mouth of the ancient man nearly smiled. He sharpened and pointed his three spears, each three-barbed and shiny at the tips, and he talked to the dog.

"Ah, we goin for carp, old dog. You like old Gerber then; you gonna come up and lick his hand when you smell carp cooking. I gonna feed you carp guts, dog, and I gonna eat carp. Ya, you like old Gerber then." He spent a half day fingering the spear edges, sharpening the tips with a tiny sharpening stone, the stone as thick and as black as his second finger, and the wary and fearful dog lay six feet from him, the dog resting his head on his forepaws, his eyes steadily watching old Gerber. The dog had become as black and muddy as Gerber, the mud clotted in the hair of the animal so that great lumps swayed beneath his belly like black grotesque teats when he walked. The mud had flattened his hair and pulled his skin tight so that he appeared skinned and dirty and yet somehow alive.

Dahlman came by and stood off, so he could not smell the old man or the dog. "The top of your shanty is sticking out of the water again," he said. "You'll be able to go home one of these days, real soon."

"Ya, my old house still there." He looked up at Dahlman and wheezed a little, his eyes wicked and black and wise, blinking like bugs on his face, and then he choked and coughed and spat. "Been through seven floods, but she still stand."

"It must be better built than it looks."

"Your grandpa help me build it. He was a good man." The faint enunciation of the "he" and the wheeze again. Old bastard, Dahlman thought, remembering how Gerber liked to reveal to him how much better the old man had been and the grandfather before him.

"Your grandpa and your pa used to eat carp with me. You want me to bring your missus a mess of carp?"

"No," Dahlman said, thinking distastefully of the soft pulp-fleshed meat of the sluggish fish, thinking too he would not even eat it if it were the most superb of fish.

"You don't like to have some, eh? The dog and me gonna have carp, eh dog?" He poked the spear at the dog, but the dog jerked away, collecting itself like some mudded skinned fish and springing back. "Yeh, he like carp guts. Gonna feed him good tonight." Looking at Dahlman again, "Maybe I bring you some carp anyway, if I catch lots."

Gerber drug on his hip boots, which were not his size, boots that were once Dahlman's father's, and which Gerber had stolen but insisted the father had given him, and were bagged and too long. He pulled himself up like some too heavy, too weighty thing of another era, and he trudged off, taking the three spears and the one gunny sack for the fish.

The dog slunk along behind.

In mid-afternoon the pacing Dahlman plunged once again out of the house, across the yard, through the muck of the cattle yard where the docile mud-splattered cattle lodged against the hot, mud-sided barn. Dahlman heard the dog whining at the edge of the water, and the dog itself was so flung with mud that it could not be seen except by its frantic movements. Dahlman thought in that moment that Gerber had teased the dog into the water or had thrown it there, but the dog was scuttling back and forth like some half-drowned sewer rat and once or twice it waded into the water up to its knees before it retreated. There was nothing in the water but the trash and the floating, still cornstalks, and farther out the sodden black trees lodged in its length in the mud and water, the tree perhaps forty yards out from where the dog was.

The dog whined and touched the ground with its nose and pointed its muzzle excitedly over the water and walked back and forth, looking out beyond the tree.

"Where's Gerber?" Dahlman asked no one. There was no movement anywhere.

And then he heard the sound, a slight splashing and a gargling out there in the mucky water, the water with its gray glitter like an oil slick where the sun reflected, and he saw the wooden tip of a spear floating in a slight arc and the head of the spear was beneath the water, heavier and weighted there. Twenty yards beyond the tree and well to the side the spear circled, and around it tiny ripples on the blinding water. Dahlman could see then too Gerber's black and greasy coat riding gently on the water.

It came to him instantly that something had gone wrong, that Gerber had been cut down while plowing around in that soft mud and that he lay out there, dead, or drowning.

"Gerber," he shouted, screeched really, for his voice was very strange. A quick, tense charge railed through him. Perhaps Gerber was indeed dead and what he had wished for several days before had come true, and that thought frightened and thrilled him. "Gerber," he shouted again, more modulated, and then there was that gargling, snuffled sound of struggle out there beyond the trees.

"The old son of a bitch," Dahlman said. "Goes out there and can't make it and I have to go pull him out." He waited as if suspended there, knowing then that he had made the decision and he did not know why he made it, and he thought, well he would do it this once, just this one time, because . . . well . . . he was young and Gerber did not have long to live anyway. His heart was beating very fast. "Gerber," he shouted. "Come out of there. Come out, you hear!"

He could see the slight motion, a swaying in the water near the sodden clump of oiled coat, and the ripples of light on that sheen of water. The dog beside Dahlman turned in frantic circles and whined and muzzled towards the water, but the older dread held him back.

Dahlman swore. He threw down the empty basket he carried and waded out. The slope of the land was very gradual, and he could see the stubs of cornstalks at intervals sticking through the water surface. The earth beneath was soft so that Dahlman sank to his ankles with each step. Gradually, as it deepened, he could feel the slide of water into his overshoes, about his feet and socks. It became a struggle to move as his overshoes filled.

"He wears the hip boots he stole from my father," he muttered. "He wears hip boots and goes out spearing but I got to go pull him out." He lifted his voice. "Gerber, get out of there! Get out, you hear me!" And more softly, "Probably nothing wrong with him anyway; probably down in the mud scraping around for gar." And saying it he knew that there was within him a rare excitement as he had never felt before, sharp and good.

He could count the old corn ridges in the mudded water, each ridge with its rotting but still hard rows of stalks three feet and six inches from the next. He measured the distance that way for thirty rows. The water deepened around the drifted tree and he knew well the little dip the land took there and he thought it had been the best land and the tree was on it now and it would have to be pulled away, perhaps cut up first so the tractor could handle the parts to be dragged out.

Gerber lay upon the water. His legs were clumped into the mud and his body was bent forward at the hips and his upper trunk floated easily. His coat spread out on the water like some scab on that vast dirty and putrid shining sore. Dahlman pulled himself out of the sucking mud step by step the last few yards to Gerber's side.

"Come on up," he said, pulling at the shoulders that moved like meal, wet and sticky from the old grease and new mud on the old man. Gerber slid down, out of Dahlman's grasp, the water-filled boots bending and pulling him, and Dahlman struggled to hold him erect. Gerber still held the used polished spear at mid-shaft and the tip was dug into the mud beside his boots.

"Come up," Dahlman said again, propping his legs beneath the old man's belly. The face was slimed with mud, and beneath that mud was a grayness such as one sees on the skin of animal carcasses, but there was a froth of bubbles on the old man's chin. Dahlman unwound Gerber's fingers from around the spear shaft and he tried to hoist the carcass upon his shoulders but the water and mud were too heavy and all he could do was to prop one arm of Gerber's around his own shoulders and drag him along.

"Come on, damn you," he said. The water was hip deep and the mud was very soft and he sank to his ankles with each step, and it was heavy labor. His overshoes were filled with water and the weight of them alone was enough to stagger anyone plowing as he did through mud and stumbling over cornstalks, but to carry a man too was an agony. He felt the sweat claw down his cheeks and back and he was very hot and he said, "Come on, damn you, old man, come on." He pulled the gray-faced, ancient creature, foul-smelling if Dahlman could have smelled then, but Dahlman's mouth was gasping breath, he pulled the ugly lump through the ugly sun-bright water and his boots made heavy sodden squirching sounds. He stumbled near the tree and fell and the weight of the old man and the water-soaked clothing all came down onto his back and he fell into the water and he had the taste of foulness and that mud-slime. He could not stand up and he struggled to his knees through an eternity of trying to lift his head and it was as if all the weight of the old man had fallen upon his neck. He reached forward clutching at the horizontal-laying trunk of the tree and fingernailed the roughness of the old and rotting bark and finally his head reached air against the old man's weight. He snarled a curse but it was lost in the bubbles in the water as his head disappeared and reappeared again, rat-like, like Gerber's ashen head, and he clawed his way up the back of the tree trunk trying to stand and finally he did stand. The mud was in his eyes and nose and ears and he could not really see or hear and he jerked angrily the ungiving weight of Gerber higher and the unbalance shoved him over. He clutched the tree for support again and he felt the cold and writhing foreign desperate aliveness, as if he had touched something always foul and evil, like the living, writhing guts of a sow, and there was a flash and the stab into his upper arm and the roiling angry cluster fighting him and the stab again lower down. His hand unclutched the snake and he heard the snapping whirr then, tiny, like a child's toy, and the elongated flash like the snap of a rubber band or the cracking jump of a mouse-trap, so quick and hitting him again. Every moment had stretched itself and time suspended as he watched with cold uncomprehension, and his first thought was, unbelievingly, the snake is so small. The snake, slender, less than two feet long, slid backward along the tree trunk top, coiling and retreating along the bark where it had been as long as it had found refuge there, the snake afraid and infuriated too at that violation, dreading the water and rolling with the floating tree trunk to the middle of the farmer's field, there to be gripped by the hard mud hand. Dahlman was frozen there, his hand still stretched out and he looked at the snake in unblinking concentration. It was a timber rattler, he thought clinically, detachedly, a snake which never grows big and which frequents the low and weedy spots of ground, a rattler a couple of years old, dark and mottled and mad with hatred and disturbance and vengeance. He watched the snake retreat up to the bark-bare broken stub of limb where it could retreat no farther, and it coiled, still trying to retreat but not able to.

Dahlman felt the fire in his arm, a kind of quickening needle warmth, the first charge being the worst, burning up to his shoulder so quickly, and he waited there, the burden of old Gerber on his other arm. He tried to calm himself and tried to think, and he thought, he was a peaceable farmer, a good quiet man, and he had done most things rightly and fairly, and every goddamn thing went wrong at once, and he wished for a moment that he had someone there to complain to, to tell exactly as it happened that he had wanted none of it and deserved none. He thought, too, of why he had ever left the yard or the house, if he had just stayed in the house old Gerber would have peacefully died and he, Dahlman, would not have been there, nor would he have heard the dog or touched the snake. And at the next moment he was enraged, and he had a sudden urge to leap upon that snake and to crush it in his fists, grind it into a writhing and rubbery powder beneath his grip, beat it into mangled shreds, beat it and beat it, and he thought that really he would have, but the weight of Gerber was too heavy on him. He stood holding his breath, feeling that burden of old Gerber on his arm and shoulder as if lodged there forever, and the building fire in his other arm from the snake stabs and both were strengthening at once, the weight and the poison fire.

"If I should leave Gerber here," he said, thinking aloud to himself, "perhaps I could make it . . ." It was now no more than thirty yards. He remembered from his school days that exertion after a snake bite was bad and that it would spread the poison quickly through him, and if he carried Gerber on there would only be exertion. If he let Gerber fall . . . released himself from that weight . . . for all he knew the old man was dead anyway. He remembered the old animosity, the bafflement and irritation of three generations of Dahlmans. Let him drop there, the water would accept old Gerber as readily as it had always reached out for him down there at his swamp shack.

From the edge of the water came the barking of the dog and whining, and the dog's high sound merged with a ringing in his ears.

Dahlman did not even look at the dog, did not look at anything for the sun was far too bright on that dark water and there was growing a terrible hotness in his head. He shoved the weight of the old man ahead of him along the tree, and he remembered vaguely that the snake had retreated the other way and they were all right. "Come on, come on," he muttered, grinding his teeth in his fury. A little froth appeared on the corners of Dahlman's mouth and his jaw was working as his legs and arms worked. He was very hot and the dizziness crept along his spine to the back of his head and he had to blink to see at all.

"Come on." He hefted the old man, pulled him nearly upright, and then he plunged past the tree into the thigh-deep water, dragging Gerber by the arms and the coat. Dahlman stumbled on the tough and tangled cornstalks submerged in mud and he fell, flailing backward, and struggled up to swallow mud and then the air and he grabbed the slipping Gerber again and pulled him on with an outraged rush, dragging him on ferociously, as a mad and bedraggled dog would drag some black, offal-stuffed rat, the legs of Gerber slithering behind, leaving a little wake of bubbles and mud.

"Come on, you old bastard, come on." Dahlman looked ahead,

but the sun was swimming in the film of muddy water and he was dizzy and he could not see and he started to vomit, but the tightness in his chest was too intense and all that he coughed was a little saliva. He closed his eyes tightly so that he could not see at all and he went on. He felt the old rows of corn in the mud and he counted them, and he lost count for the ringing in his ears and yet he went on, until the blood thundered in his skull and twisted his brain so that his eyes seemed to leave their very sockets, were wrenched aside too, distorted as his whole body was rent and distorted. The dog barked nearer, farther, nearer, louder and louder, the dog going mad in its panic, and Dahlman clenched his face and tried to run, dragging the slithering Gerber like a turtle through the mud and he fell and felt the water splash and the water did not even cover his knees. He clutched ahead and found the barking dog. His hands caught the dog and he pulled himself ahead and he and Gerber and the sprawling, yelping dog were rolling together, and Dahlman swore over and over with the blood choking him, "Damn you, Gerber. Damn you."

There was the high cry of the woman, and Dahlman saw the convulsive sun vibrate and the earth yawned and opened and the world burned him in its jerking convulsive motion.

The Right Hand

The boy stood tense, holding the post steady and straight in the post hole his father had dug to fill the broken line in the fence. He was a young boy, twelve or so, with light blond hair, like his father's where it had not turned gray, and with eyes the color of smoke, holding the even cool color in his eyes as he looked across the hill into the valley where the neighbor lived. The boy watched the neighbor come slowly up the hill, across the cornstalk-littered ground, turning now deeply but sparsely green with the new spring crop of oats. The neighbor was still a long way away, but the boy scrutinized him closely as he approached.

They had come there in the spring; the boy's father and the family of six, not counting the mother, had come to this cold farm with its spiny trees like thistles and the old, unpainted buildings crouched between two hills like broad-backed snuffing gray-colored hogs. The boy had come with his parents and his five brothers and sisters, but for two months he had seen no stranger except at the country school—only his father had visited around, talking to the neighbors and returning home to tell what the neighbors knew.

The cows broke out the day before, snapped the rusted wires and the rotted posts that harbored fat white slugs and the sawdust manure of wood-boring bugs, and had trampled across the neighbor's oats field, chewing up the harrowed land turning green with young oats with their hooves, before the boy and his father got them turned back. The cows were still in the yard and he and his father worked on the fence, putting the posts in first before the wires could be pulled up and repaired. The day was cloudy, portending rain, and the clouds slid fast from behind one gray hill, over them, to the other hills beyond, drizzling lightly, only to be told by the sensitive pricks on bare arms, leaving a coldness like a snake-skin chill.

"Kick in some dirt, Clayton. Don't just stand there," the father said with a voice thick and slow but still reflecting a kind of impatience. The boy looked down to the half-moon slit around the post and pushed some dirt into the hole with his foot. The father told him to stop then, and he bent, kneeling beside the post, and tamped the dirt tight and hard. The old man used a long, slender steel rod to tamp the dirt in. The boy watched the arm and the steel rod pump up and down, leisurely but powerfully, saw the sweated shirtsleeves move with the slow, strong movements of the old man.

"There's a man coming up the hill," the boy said. The old man did not say anything. He acted as if he hadn't heard.

"There's a man coming," the boy said again, insistently.

"I know," the father said, his voice flat with indifference. "I seen him an hour ago. Now pass in some more dirt."

The boy pushed in the dirt and watched the man come to them, the shoes of the man heavy in the mud of the new oats field.

"Howdy," the man said, when he was near to them, and the father turned on his knees and laid the bar aside.

"Howdy," the old man said, grasping the post and standing with

heaviness and tiredness. The father squinted at the face of the neighbor, hidden partly behind the pulled-down cap, while the boy
gawked at it. It was a face bloodless and yet suffused with a blood
color, a face with a scraped lavender birthmark, the mark starting
at the temple, hidden partly by the cap, and cutting down the left
side of the face from the ear to the jawbone and fringed at the lips
with the deep-purple shade, the color of a rotted plum that the
worms have eaten into, and the mark branded the eye with a living,
livid, sore redness, making anyone who saw the man look instinc-
tively at the inflamed texture around the left eye. The birthmark
pulled the lips crooked, made them seem open, even if they were
not, made them look dead with that deep-purple, bloodless,
blooded color. It was the purple of something dead—the purple on
dead horses' heads before the rendering truck or hogs come to
them. The boy stared at this face, the face reflecting the sorrow and
the sufferings of lifetimes, a face with the mark of Cain perhaps, or
just of the man's parents; it was a face with that naked hurting look
of a burn or a brand healing and yet never quite healed, always
inflamed and sensitive and sore; it was a face of terror and of bad
dreams, giving to anyone who saw it a weird and evilfearing anxiety.

"You're Ezra Stark," the father said.

They both—the boy and the father—watched the lips of Ezra
Stark to see if they were alive, if the purple face and the drooping
red-bordered eye were something living or dead.

"Yes," Stark said, his lips hardly moving, and he looked at the
boy, but the boy did not notice the eyes; he only saw the inflamed
worm-lavender cheek and the sagging corner of the raw mouth.

"I was over to your place the other day," the father said. "But
there was nobody home."

"I must have been in the field," Stark said. There was a faint lisp
in his voice, a faint struggle to form words and speak. He spoke
very slowly, and his voice was deep.

"We're just putting up the fence," the father went on. "My cows busted out."

"I seen the oats field," Stark said. He looked at the gawking boy again, studied the boy's face a moment and looked away, at the old man again. The father noticed the boy then, too.

"What you looking at, boy?" he said. "You never seen a stranger before? You can finish up this post—that'll give you something to do while men talk."

The boy knelt obediently and pushed dirt into the black half-moon and tamped the clods, crushing them, sealing the post in.

The boy felt a shudder—it was not the air and the wisps of drizzle. He knew what it was—there was evil here. He had a swift recognition of the evil of something warped, the terror of darkness and the strange; he had felt it before, on cold lightning-fired nights, in the chill of the church on Sunday mornings, on entering an unlighted barn. This had always held a secret terror for him, for he went much to Sunday school and church, and he had heard much of evil, had known it to be rampant and secret, and it had always been hidden secretly from him, behind bannisters on stairs, in the darkness of doorways at church, behind corners cringing in barns, in the dank, tree-overhung lagoons that were nursed with bad water and a stench down along the river. It had always been a secret terror for him before, but now it was here, very near to him; he could look up and see the heavy, mudded shoetops of the neighbor with that face strange, carved as if from red and rotted wood with the purple, bloodless leer and the red-rimmed, gouged eye.

The boy breathed quickly, not so much from the work, placing the post, as from the quick fear and hot, nerve-catching fascination of being so near to that which he had feared and had always wanted to see, face to face, all his life, but had never seen until now.

The boy moved his slight shoulders and patted the earth, smoothing it carefully around the post. He knelt and looked from beneath his blue cap bill at Stark, at the man with the hideous evil face. He wondered what the man thought, if there were evil thoughts, plans, sweeping through him, like spiders crawling inside that reddened skull, and if the spiders too had that cold and dead and bloodless purple look, like rotted plums. He thought of it and felt the sudden fascination and hatred come over him again. He was afraid to look at the man's face, looking instead at the heavy mud-laden shoes, hearing the voices of his father and Stark speak from a distance.

His father did most of the talking; he was always one for that, never missing an opportunity to visit even if no one else wanted to talk, as they did not want to around this, their new place. His father talked of oats and went to scrabble in the wet dirt to look for seed that hadn't sprouted, and the man, Stark, followed him, and stood in half-crouched posture, bent from the waist, as if he were hardly interested in what the father did. The boy watched him now, watched with a calm intensity, expecting the man to do something, violent and sudden, and if he did the boy knew what he would do; he would spring to the aid of his father in that struggle, he would swing the long steel bar, he saw it now—the swift, crushing, sodden violence, and the fine muscles in his arms grew rigid in preparation, but the man did not do anything at all.

The man, Stark, went away then, down the long slope towards the shack and the outbuildings partly hidden by trees, partly by the hills, moving with heavy, mud-laden feet, pulling up the oats turf worse than any cow had done.

"He has a bad scar," the father said to the boy. They went to the next post, and the father dug the spade in and turned the earth out, preparing to make the hole.

"What did he get it from? Did he always have it?" the boy asked.

"It's a birthmark," the father said. "He never goes anyplace because of it. I'm surprised he came up here to talk to us today."

"He probably had a reason," the boy said, with faint insinuation.

"What reason?" the father asked, gasping with the work of the auger. "Oh, the cows—no, he wasn't mad about that. He didn't even mention it."

The boy listened to his father and knew the old man did not understand as he understood.

———————◦—◁▷—◦———————

The boy could move like a shadow or like smoke, noiseless and swift, more often not moving at all, standing silent, blending in with where he stood. He had learned it hunting with his father, had learned to stalk rabbits and squirrels and an occasional rare deer, moving as silent as smoke through the woods, blending by his careful tenseness into the trees and the corn. Sometime when he was younger—it was on another farm, another time—he had recognized his ability to be silent, to tread with smoke softness, and he could come nearly to neighbors' yards and there he squatted and watched and listened and when he was satisfied he drifted off again. He was quiet, the boy; he told no one of what he did or what he had seen or heard—he knew much, for he heard many of the intimate and violent man-and-wife arguments of his neighbors—knew more than the neighbors would ever admit aloud, and no one ever questioned him. There were six in the family and he was the third, and they were all too busy to notice him except when they needed him for work or chores—milking or egg gathering. The boy helped with the chores on summer evenings, milking down in the hot, fly-infested barn, and then, later, he sat in the wooden chair by the yellow kerosene lamp in what was called the living room, although the only thing that made it different from the kitchen was that it had no stove and dinner table, and there he dutifully did his catechism work. He was to be confirmed in the church in the spring, and it was important that he know his lessons of devoutness and godliness, and his mother listened to him recite before he could go out again.

The summer nights were thick with hotness and liquid heaviness, giving the evening a warm, oily texture like warm bacon grease, airless in the hollows between the hills where the corn grew lush and tall, crowded with the small, intimate sounds of locusts and crickets, sounds that mixed and settled in the hot, pollen-laden air, but jarred somehow by the strangeness and loudness of human voices and the slamming of doors far away. The evenings lingered, dusty and quiet and warm, lingered in a dusty lethargy, like a fat and squashed too-ripe pear silked over with dust.

The boy moved then, after his Bible history and catechism lessons, drifted like smoke across the barbed fence, hardly raising a sound, and across the road to the other fence and was submerged in the cornfield. He followed the corn row down the hill, moving with alacrity and swiftness and utter stillness, with less sound than the bees above the cornfield or the rustle of the blue-green bayonet leaves themselves, which no one ever hears consciously, and he stepped carefully from foxtail clump to clump, so that there were only a few random footprints in the dirt.

He came at last to the farmstead, to the bleak, unpainted buildings in the hollow. The boy slid on his belly along the fence until he came at last to a stop in the shadow of brush that had once been a plum thicket and there he squatted and watched the yard. The house was near to him, on his left, and to his right stood the gray outbuildings, the barn and the corncrib and granary and chickenhouse. It took the boy a moment to sense where Stark was; he listened and turned his head carefully until at last he recognized the faint sounds of movement in the barn. Stark was milking. The boy squatted and clasped his hands between his knees and waited.

He had come there many times, to this spot or to places near it, and he had waited and watched. He was never impatient, and sometimes he did not see anything and at other times he saw much. He remembered especially, clearly, the time Stark brought the basket full of movement up from the hog yard. The boy saw the wet slimy head of a newborn calf over the edge of the basket as Stark carried it up, and the boy wondered why he carried the calf to the house. He saw for a moment incantations, weird magic in firelight, sacrifices of newborn calves with blood dripping endlessly from slashed, furred throats, all this and more behind the sagging screen door of Stark's house. The light came on in the backroom where the shades were always pulled—the boy had learned quickly that Stark always went there soon after sundown and lit the lamp, making the tan, always-pulled shades glow with a weak yellow color, and then there was a light, too, in a nearer, a front room, that must have been the kitchen, but there was no other movement and no other sound, and then the lights were extinguished, first the front one and then the one in the backroom and there was nothing else at all, no light, no sound. The boy slid down the little slope until he knelt by the porch, but still he heard and saw and smelled nothing. It was as if all living creatures had vanished from around him and he was utterly alone. It terrified him and fascinated him, as seeing Stark that first day had done. He returned night after night, intent on seeing the calf; he changed his vantage point until he was certain it must still be in the house, or perhaps in Stark himself, or perhaps still bleeding as some evil sacrifice to a terrible, purplefaced, livid god. And then one day he saw the calf again, saw Stark lead it out, his hands under the calf's belly, quite gently, across the porch, and the calf could not

walk, and it tried to stand and could not and it collapsed, bellow-
ing a strange, squeaky and broken half-wit bellow. The boy understood then; he had seen newborn calves chewed by hogs, and he
knew this calf had its forefeet chewed off to nubs, and Stark had
wrapped the feet, and the bandages were red with iodine and
sticky with some khakicolored poultice. Stark lifted the calf and
set it carefully in the grass and weeds flanking the house, folding
the calf's struggling legs so it would lie down, but the calf kept
trying to stand up and would not lie down, even when Stark was
there holding it. Stark tried to feed it with a bottle, but it would
not take the nipple. Later on, the animal tired from its violent
struggle to stand, and Stark came out in the late-evening gloom
after the milking and he was able to feed it a little, but it was appar-
ent to the boy, who had often trucked out dead pigs and chickens
and even calves to the fields to rot, that the calf would die, and
yet Stark tried to feed it and keep it alive. It was all like something
mad, something utterly fierce and crazy, the way the gaunt, disfigured man came out and struggled with the weak, dying calf
and tried to feed and nourish it. When Stark was not there on
later evenings the animal tried to rise, and it fell on its side, and
rose again, and it undid the bandages in its threshings and the
white, hard nubs of the bones stood out like something naked
and hurting and polished whitely, like ivory, and the boy thought
"kill it, kill it" with a fury at the man who would want to keep
such a thing alive, but still Stark tried to feed it and nourish it and
he replaced the bandages and lathered them heavily with Vase-
line. After two days the calf would not eat anymore and even then
somehow it managed to stand, its sides transparent against the
toothpick, tiny-slat ribs, and it wandered thus, falling and rising
and floundering in the dust of the yard, like some mad tormented
creature, driven by something inexplicable and terrible, seeking
to hide in the shade of the plum brush, but always falling and

being drawn in the wrong direction, wandering, mad and awful, disfigured and torn, yet somehow, madly, relentlessly living, driven like its master to live, in spite of the want for death, until at last it did die, with even the last death motion feeble, and the calf bellow only a gurgle in the quivering throat, and in the evening when the dust had cooled and Stark came back in from the fields, he took the calf and carried it up the pasture hill and buried it. The boy could see the place where he went quite clearly from where he watched.

After that the boy had even a deeper terror of and hatred for Stark. It was not because of the calf; he had no sympathy for it, for he had seen suffering, he had witnessed agony and seen the dumb struggling eyes of animals in pain, and he had grown used to it, had felt nothing at seeing death—no, that was not it—it was that Stark could want something so misshapen, so awful around, and would want to make it live. The boy wanted to destroy the calf the first time he saw it because it was so badly disfigured, just as he had calmly destroyed ducklings with misshapen beaks and pigs that were born with their guts outside themselves. That which was misshapen and marked was evil, was not natural, and needed to be destroyed, and he felt a shudder run through him, remembering how Stark wanted to keep the animal alive. There was something terrible in that effort at prolonging the life of something already wrongly there.

Stark had finished milking and he came across the yard from the barn, carrying the pail in one hand and the lantern in the other and the lantern made the shadows of his legs appear black and huge, swaying jerkily as he walked. Stark disappeared into the house, and again the light in the backroom came on first. The boy edged along the fence row behind the house until he squatted only six feet from the window with the yellow, drawn shades. There was no sound; nothing. He wondered about the light, what it could mean, why it was so important that a light burn there whenever it was dark. Perhaps, he thought, Stark was really not alone; a thousand thoughts swung through him, and he bent his head to listen but there was still no sound, no movement. He heard the locusts in the trees and the friendly crickets and then Stark turning the cream separator in the kitchen, and then the separator, too, was silent. The boy heard the door slam and he knew Stark was going out to feed the calves the skim milk. The boy stood up and moved back towards the plum thicket. It was completely dark now and he moved by ear, and it was then, as he came to the corner of the house, that he sensed someone, even as the other person, startled, sensed his presence, and the boy threw himself back as the hands reached towards him, clutching his shirt, tearing it.

"Who are you?" Stark said, his voice loud and near, and the hands tore for him, but the boy was very quick and he ducked, turning all at once, and he hit the fence and doubled over it, feeling quick pain cut him and forgetting it as he was up and running again. At the top of the hill he stopped and listened. It was dead silent. He stood, breathing hard, pausing in his breathing to listen, and tried to figure what had happened. Stark had been surprised, too, he knew, probably more surprised than he. When it was light he would come up the hill, following the tracks. The boy felt ashamed, for he had prided himself on his quickness and quietness and cleverness, too, and to be nearly caught was something to feel ashamed about. Perhaps Stark was clever too, he thought, and this made him feel better. It was a kind of contest now, a contest of wits and observation that it had not been before. He caught his breath and then doubled back, and turned and went down the hill away from both the Stark place and his own, making firm tracks, and when he reached the bottom where there were trees and grass, he walked carefully and lightly up to the road, and then crossed the road, brushing out his tracks behind him. After he crossed the road he was in their own pasture again, and he walked quickly up the hill to the house.

He did not go down to the Stark place for several days after that, but finally something drove him back; it was a curiosity, a compulsion. He wanted to know about Stark, about the lighted backroom; he wanted to see again and watch again and he wanted to feel the fear and tenseness and the terror. He knew he wanted that—the terror and the disgust, and yet somehow he hated it too; he wanted to feel the hatred and shuddering disgust burn through him, and still he wanted to destroy it. It was this that drew him back; it was something like the pleasure of hunting, of fearing to kill something and still wanting very much to kill; it was like the sweet feeling of bringing death—death to something that shouldn't or needn't live except as a target for a rifle.

He chose his vantage point differently this time, moving between two box elder trees, protected from the yard by the battered sway-sided hump of a collapsed garage, but still able to see the yard quite clearly. He was only a few yards from the backroom where the light came on and then, that evening, the front door slammed and he saw Stark moving, lantern and pail in hand, to the barn, his legs throwing great grotesque shadows as he moved.

After he had passed out of sight, the boy moved, with the lightness of smoke, across the weed-patch yard to beside the yellow window. He tried the window but it was tight, locked from the inside. The boy hesitated. He knew he must see the room, see what was there. Again he felt the swift thrill of terror and excitement, if he should be seen or if he should get caught, come face to face with the lavender scar and the redrimmed eye. He circled the house and waited to see if Stark was anywhere in sight, but then he saw the lantern swaying down in the yards. The boy moved soundlessly across the porch and swung open the screen door. The kitchen was dark; he knew it was the kitchen by the soured odor of the cream separator and by the heavy smell of fried potatoes. He went quickly through the room and through another one to the room with the lamp. He stopped and looked about him. It was only a bedroom, quite neat and clean, with a bed and a dresser and a chest of drawers. The lamp stood on the dresser and beside it were some slender books, a half dozen or so, with titles the boy had never seen before, and there was a picture, too, of a family. The boy looked at it; it was the only thing to look at in the room. It was an old picture, taken years before, quite yellow now. The man sitting rigidly in the straight chair with arms folded across his chest had on a stiff celluloid collar, and the woman had a frowzy, tormented look on her face. In the picture, too, were a boy and a girl, the boy younger, both plain, vacant-faced children, like any other boy and girl. And on the picture, written very faintly, but carefully, too, as if it had been written a long time before, above the man's head were the words "Ezra Stark, Sr., died 1938," and above the woman's "Mathilda Stark, died 1943," and "Carl" beside the boy, and "Harriet" beside the girl. He did not know why the picture was there, and he did not really care.

The boy surveyed the room again. He was genuinely disappointed. He had expected something of a purpose perhaps, overwhelming and evil, a mad old woman, an opium den, a room full of glowering icons, but instead there was only the single dull picture. He turned to go when he caught the swift light sound of a step on the porch. The boy felt a swift clutch of fear—the windows were no good, the bed too low. Now that he was inside, in a strange room, he felt trapped and confused—outside, with space and movement, he could think and act, but here, here he did not know where to turn. He pulled the closet curtain back and stepped inside, burrowing beneath some coats hung on the bar above his head. The curtain trembled after his movement and he tried to still it, but there was the faint vibration as he heard Stark come slowly from the kitchen into the room. The boy held his breath; he dared not breathe, for he could hear every breath, every movement of Stark. Now that he needed to hold his breath, every second demanded a new one. The blood flooded his temples, there was a filled choking feeling in his throat, he had to breathe but Stark was still there, and he did not breathe. He saw the silhouette of Stark against the curtain, saw Stark move across the room, and then slowly turn and go away again, and still the boy did not breathe, even with the blood pounding in his temples and his hands like ice. He heard the footsteps move away, heard the creaking of the floor in the other room and then the half-musical sprongging sound of the screen door opening and closing, and yet the boy waited, breath drawn in, until the stillness settled again, dropped with that heavy silence that could be only the silence of one alone. He moved then, looking carefully past the edge of the curtain into the lamp-lit yellow room, and then he crossed the room to the dresser. He shielded his eyes against the lamp and looked out into the late half light, half darkness, and then he turned the lock on the window and opened it. The window was very dusty and had not been cleaned for a long time. There was no screen and he shoved the window up and prepared to go out when his arm touched the lamp and jarred it and he had a quick breathless moment catching it, keeping it from falling, and then suddenly, quickly, quite deliberately, he flung the lamp on the floor, smashing it, sending kerosene and the flame eating after the kerosene across the floor and beneath the bed. It was a small blue-yellow flame at first as he watched it, growing yellowly, with a faint fuzzy orange color as the flames caught at the blankets overhanging the bed. The boy slid out the window and moved in a crouched half-run across the yard. He did not look back until he reached the hilltop in the cornfield and then the whole house was a rich cherry glow in the valley, the flames licking the roof and the sides of the house like cherry drippings on chocolate, and the boy watched, feeling the tightness in his chest from running or from fear, he did not know which.

He walked now, carefully, mocking the sounds of the late-evening doves from the trees in the pasture. He thought someday he would go hunting them. There was no one around the place when he got there; even the mother was gone. The boy slipped up to the porch, drifting in perfectly soundlessly, so that even the sleeping dog did not awaken until the boy was already in the kitchen door. The boy went into the living room and sat down in the straight chair by the lamp and opened his catechism and waited. He heard the cars go by the place, all going down towards Ezra Stark's place, and much later even a fire truck from town, and then the cars began coming back, and the mother came in the house, and looked at him, with some excitement and some surprise, and she asked where he had been; there was a fire at that old bachelor's, Stark's place, and the boy said he wondered why all the cars went by, down there.

A long while later the father and the brothers came back, and the father took off his soot-covered cap and sat down.

"It was awful," he said. "I never seen anything so awful."

"What?" the boy said.

"Wasn't you there too, boy?"

"I was studying my catechism."

The father nodded. "The fire at Stark's—it was terrible. Stark must have gone into the shack after something, I don't know what, and we found him in what used to be the bedroom. We could smell him a hundred yards away."

"Was he dead?" the boy asked, leaning forward suddenly.

"There was hardly anything left of him," the father said, "or of the house either. It was awful."

The boy felt a great warmness ride him, cover him as if honey or an anointment bathed him, as if some great evil had lifted from him, from everyone now. He would not need to go down there again; it was all finished, there was no longer anything for him to do. He closed his eyes and luxuriated in the rich, good feeling it gave him.

"It was some fire," one of the brothers said. "You should have been there to see it."

"It was terrible," the father said.

"I was studying my catechism," the boy said.

The Shooters

The brother brought the news of the killings even before dawn; he had been in to Charleston to deliver a butcher hog to the locker plant for slaughtering that day, and had run into Gavin Terrell, the young town marshal, his friend, and had heard of it—how the whole family up by Craig, not ten miles away, Jung he believed their name was (it would be on the news pretty soon), was shot to death by .22 rifle, the father of past forty, the wife, the eighty-two-year-old mother-in-law, the eleven-year-old boy, and the young hired man to boot, all shot and dumped like sacks of potatoes into the entrance of the storm cellar. Done the day before, the previous afternoon, the coroner had reported.

The brother spoke carefully, looking at the mother who was old and suffered from high blood pressure, wanting not to frighten her, but better to tell her now than wait for the hysterical news reports.

"Na, na," the mother said, "has the world gone crazy?" She sat at the kitchen table and rubbed the top with a wet cloth, preparing it for breakfast with elaborate care, as she did every day. "Why would anybody do such a thing? Crazy, that's what."

The brother shrugged.

"Do they know who did it?" Leonard's wife asked.

"No. Of course not," Leonard said, looking to the brother for verification.

"I'll bet it was a neighbor," the brother, Melvin, said. "Went off his head. Probably mad about something. Some of these neighbor troubles go back for years."

"It's common enough nowadays, people being crazy," the mother said. She began to tell of the farmers and wives who had needed psychiatrists in recent years, or had been sent up to Cherokee for a time, all from that area alone.

The young wife frowned above the frying pans on the kitchen stove where she stood preparing their early breakfast. "Do you suppose it's really just a neighbor who went mad? Or somebody on the loose? Somebody who's a killer? It seems so terrible for someone to kill five people. Just a neighbor couldn't do that, I would think."

The brothers looked at each other. Melvin, the farmer, cap on, wrestled with his hands. "Whoever it was, they'll catch him today. Might have got him already, as far as anybody knows."

"And how many were there?" the mother asked, rubbing carefully in circles on the smooth artificial table top.

"Five. Even the hired man, a kid of seventeen. Stayed there overnight because of haying. He didn't even belong there."

"Why would a neighbor take him too? I mean if it were a neighbor doing the shooting? Why the kid too?" Leonard asked.

There was a pause, a reflective moment, and the brother thinking of this new aspect that had not occurred to him.

"Yeh," he muttered, not wanting to say more.

"It's somebody crazy is all," the old mother said, finished then with the table, arising and going to the sink, collecting potatoes in a gray enameled pan, and the knife, sitting down again and beginning to peel them for the noon meal, their dinner.

"Are you going to Sioux City today?" Melvin asked.

"Yes. Every day. You know that," Leonard said. Every day since the discovery, in mid-visit to the Iowa farm where his old mother and brother lived, of cancer, and the necessity of going to Sioux City for radiation treatments, six minutes each day beneath the Cobalt-60 machine. He borrowed his brother's car each day for the thirty-four-mile trip, an hour and a half gone and back.

"You going this morning or this afternoon?" Melvin asked. Leonard looked to his wife. She lifted eggs and bacon from the skillet, tested cornbread in the oven, put that out too. No sign from her for a preference.

"This afternoon," Leonard said.

Melvin nodded. "Okay," he said. "Gavin wanted me to come into town this morning. To help out."

Leonard nodded, understanding him.

"You'll be around here all morning?" Melvin asked.

"Yes," Leonard said, knowing his brother was aware of the danger, wanting to protect the farm and the mother from being alone.

All that morning Leonard and his wife and his mother worked in the garden, not with the old mean labor that he had given when he was a boy, twenty years ago, but rather with an easy pleasantness that came from doing work that one didn't feel compelled to do; they set out tomato plants and weeded the strawberries. There were already many strawberry blossoms, fragile and white.

At noon sharp, Melvin was back.

"Well, did you and Gavin nab the killer?" Leonard asked. Melvin shook his head, grinned. "Nope. There's a story they got somebody up at Spencer. But nobody's sure yet, and Gavin doesn't believe it."

At one o'clock they went to Sioux City. No, the mother did not want to go along. "Ooph, I'm not feeling so good today," she said, Leonard thinking she was only begging off to have her afternoon nap. They drove the new highway, thirty-four miles in thirty minutes, went in to see the sleepy radiologist who muttered of palliation. "Are you feeling all right now?"

"Yes," Leonard said.

"No back pain anymore?"

"No."

"He gets tired very easily," the wife said.

"Yes. That's bound to happen," the radiologist said, and gave a stricken yawn, trapped it partially between throat and chin. "That's caused by the radiation. But your back pain has gone away?"

"Yes."

"Good. Good."

They, the sleepy doctor and the robust nurse, took him through the heavy lead door and lay him on the cot, rolled him beneath a streamlined bullet-shaped machine that said "Eldorado" on it.

"Only two more treatments on your side and then we radiate your neck," the doctor said. "That will suppress the growth, and give palliation for a good long time."

The thought of time, any time, gave him a chill, how the bored doctor could talk easily of a "good long time" when he knew it could not be more than three years at the most for him, this doctor who could easily yawn away three years of his own life without even thinking about it.

Leonard did not say anything. He lay still, as he should, looked up at the perforated squares on the ceiling, lay silent in the air-conditioned comfort of the lead-in room. The red light came on after the radiologist and nurse exited to the safety of their control booth, the machine above him thukked and a little complacent hum of the machine began, as of a digestive process deep within it. He contemplated lying there, and of the discovery three weeks before of the malignant cancer in him, not localized, spread already with unseemly haste, and where the doctors had at first talked confidently of energetic treatment and suppression, now their lips could manage murmurs of only "palliation," an unforgivable word to him, absolutely a devilish word to him at thirty-three. Palliation and defeat, and nothing to be done, oh the best doctors agreed, there was nothing else to be done, for "it" had already spread beyond localized bounds, and what was there now to do but palliate and wait?

He waited the six minutes, felt nothing but the hard cot beneath him, heard nothing but the mystery of the tiny hum, looked at the perforations, little holes in the ceiling, clean as if made by tiny bullets, and the efficient gamma rays burned into his bowels, warmed his kidneys, all unfeeling. The curved machine thukked exactly on time, the red light went out, the nurse forced open the heavy door and came in smiling, wheeled him from under.

In somber quiet, as usual now on this, the eighteenth trip to and from radiation, they shot the thirty-four miles back to Charleston, needed nothing in the little town, saw Gavin Terrell camped strategically in the police car at the edge of town, waved to him. Gavin waved back, smiled.

"They haven't got him yet," Leonard said, the first words in all that way.

"How do you know?" his wife asked.

"Gavin wouldn't be sitting there if they had."

They went the two and a half miles to the farm and down the long lane from the gravel road.

"Oh, the cattle are down this way!" the wife said, delighted, and it was true, the large herd spread on both sides of the creek, near the farmstead. "We've got to take some pictures."

"That will be nice," he said, the sullenness still on him.

The brother, Melvin, and the old hired man who came whenever Melvin needed him worked on the seeder; there were soybeans to be replanted and the seeder was pulled in the middle of the yard.

"The cattle are down this way," the wife said to them. "Is it all right if I take some pictures of them?"

"Take as many as you want," Melvin said, getting up from under the machine and looking himself. The pasture was a mile long, and narrow, for it flanked the creek on both sides. The cattle were young and tended toward wildness, newly brought from the Nebraska range. The first thing they'd done after the 160 head had been unloaded was to go to the far end of the pasture, the mile away, and herd up there. Melvin had explained it to them when they went out to count the cattle one time. "The only experience they've had with barns and buildings is with things that hurt, vaccination, castration, branding, and so naturally they want to stay away from anything that looks like buildings."

And they had until now.

"Well maybe the grass is getting short up at the other end," Melvin said, although he knew and Leonard knew that could not be.

The wife was excited and pleased. She got the camera and went out by the fence and the beautiful Hereford calves lifted their heads and sniffed, and she took the picture, with at least a hundred heads, white-faced and white ears, pointing at her.

"I thought I'd never get a picture of them," she said, back at the yard, pleased with everything.

Leonard sat on the porch and slipped the oiled cloth along the spine of the Marlin rifle. Sullenly he cleaned the gun, although he had cleaned it the day before after shooting the six pigeons up at the other place that Melvin farmed. He knew that he was sullen, and told himself he could not help it, could not. The bandage on his neck bothered him, the bandage covering the latest biopsy only three days old. He cranked his head and touched the wad on his neck.

"Don't pull at that, please, Len," his wife said.

"Aaah," he muttered, slipped the cloth the length of the rifle, noted appreciatively the steel gleam, the hard steel bolt reflecting neither figure nor shadow, only light.

"Aah," he muttered again, touching the lump of bandage with his fingertips. The cold lumps of frozen things in himself, those lumps of growing cancers, and the hot unhealthy burn of the radiation, neither good, he thought, both or either would kill him, frozen and burning all at once, and if he thought of it he could feel them both, he believed, truly feel them crawl in his tissues, in his marrow, that dark cold cancer in him and the glow of the radiation; condemned to death quite surely, and he did not know how or why. Nor did anyone.

Snap! the bolt went shut, beautiful, slick and sliding elegantly the Marlin .22 that he had cleaned up and made good again. The shining steel-colored bolt slipped open and shut and open again beneath his finger touch. He looked down the barrel and the beautiful grooves spiraling down to the distant small opening where the small bullet entered, and closed the bolt.

"Think I'll get a pigeon or two," he said by way of explanation to the women, his wife working with the flowers in the front yard, his mother sitting in the lawn rocking chair. He took the new box of bullets, fingered out six and filled the clip, snapped the clip in, liked the way the bolt slid forward, seated the slender little bullet, closed solidly. Now truly a weapon.

"Na, there he goes again," the mother said, "shooting birds and rabbits. Murderer," laughing a little, looking at the wife to see if she would smile.

He turned sharply on his mother, really snarled, "Mind your own business, goddamn it," feeling a ridge of blood thunder in his forehead, his arm tremble, and a burning beneath the bandage. Murderer! Murdered would be better, he thought.

"Well, Leonard," his wife said chidingly, and softly too, lest he get really angry. The mother looked away as if she had not heard; she had had five sons and had borne many ferocious asides.

He went through the gate, carrying the good-feeling rifle. The dog wanted to follow; he sent him back. In deadly quiet he moved up along the heavy windbreak, any slight sounds he had to make completely hidden by the crash and bang of the hogs feeding in the near hog yard. Beyond the box elders he heard the chattering, unmistakable, of squirrels. He wondered absently if this was a female with young, knew they were almost impossible to tell apart from the males, and he had seen a dozen or so in the last week, cavorting foolishly and openly around the corncrib. Whatever it was, it would have to take its chances, for what followed would be purely by design. He slid up in the protection of a tree, peered gingerly forward, could tell finally the movement high in a far maple, the scolding squirrel, head and body pointed straight down the trunk.

He brought the rifle up, not moving fast, careful to avoid startling motion, traced the barrel at the squirrel thirty yards away, planted the rear sight on him, on his neck, lowered the blade of the front sight so that it rested at the bottom of the rear, exactly as he had tested it from a hundred practice shots, followed the squirrel perhaps six inches or so as it came down the trunk, and worked back on the tender trigger.

Interesting, always interesting, he thought, plucking at the bandage on his neck that itched and was hot suddenly, and hurt worse after he plucked at it, interesting to see that change, the profound and remarkable alteration that the snap of one small .22 bullet could make. The birds fled, a quiet dropped on the windbreak, only the impervious hogs went on completely unaffected. The target itself, the squirrel, headed forward, still facing downward, but now as if its whole will and effort must be to return, to go upward, and the weight of ten planets sucking it with deadly force.

A sag, tail, fur, fat, everything wrinkled downward, and that enormous gravity drew it down, the pads of feet dug grimly into the bark. He thought for a moment he would have to shoot again but then with a slipping suddenness the brown squirrel skittered down the bark, crashed with astonishing heaviness into the bush beneath the tree.

The lurking dog came up and seized the squirrel, and Leonard spoke sharply, and the dog retreated. The squirrel was male, very heavy. Fed on Iowa corn, it should be, Leonard thought. The bullet had gone in an inch in back of the skull. It had been dead from the moment of the shot, he thought, and had hung on not even reflexively, only the feet thinking reflexively.

He picked it up by the tail, studied the dulled round eyes without wanting to. "Palliation," he said aloud, and threw the squirrel right at the dog. The dog hopped away, turned away from him, the animal uncertain if he were angry with him.

"Poor sensitive beast," he muttered viciously at the dog, thinking—perhaps you need palliation too, poor creature.

The woods were quiet, and very hot now. The gnats, fat and hairy and insistent, thick as miniature buffalo and shaped like them, were everywhere. Leonard went out, skirted the old machine shed, the dog coming after, forgetting the squirrel now, the dog fat and useless although not old, it ever useless, but interested in hunting, nothing could make it move as could the appearance of a gun.

"Go on, go back! Get!" The dog retreated, showing whites of eyes, one raised forepaw, its dignity wounded, it trying to save a remnant of that. It backed away. Leonard slid along the side of the barn, past the empty milking shed, and at the corner he waited, carefully, pulled in his breath, for he could hear the cooing, the pigeons always pursuing breeding, always ready for that. If he shot a dozen a day there would yet be pigeons. His brother wanted them out for they carried a host of diseases, he said. On that hint Leonard had shot many.

At the top of the barn, under the long eave where the hay trolley ran the pigeon perched, the blue head pivoted and bobbed and looked at him, and it too foolish or inexperienced to fly. The beautiful rifle arced perfectly, the little wedge of sight fastened on the blue breast with the elegant tracings of lavender, so bright, so stunning it almost hurt the eyes, like something imagined when one was young and worked with the brilliant range of colors in drawing books, and could never hope to achieve, the little needle of front sight bobbed at the lower edge, just a hint of brass touched the lavender V on the blue breast. The snap of sound, clear, washing all eardrums of fuzziness, and down it came, fluttering of bluish down, and it much faster, quick as lightning, thunked against the concrete, did not move.

He heard the frightened movement, waited, this one exit there above, the white-winged bird came out, was just on the point of its hurried and hysterical flight when he shot (his hand had changed old used bullet case for new one automatically, the greased slide, slip and motion, click nicely of steel), and thought he might have missed for an instant the way the bird did fly, but the puff of feathers told him different immediately. He waited, saw the pull of wings turn ineffectual, the flight fall lumpish, and it slammed somersaulting and rolling into the ground down there beyond the tank.

The dog whined in its anxiety to be in to them, but the gates were closed, the whining almost a whistling, it so anxious and insistent and begging.

Beyond the barn he saw the other pigeon, up on the silo in the middle of the feeding yard, a long shot for a .22 without a scope. (The rifle had had a scope when he came, but he took it off, the shots too easy with it; "what's the sense?" he'd asked, "you lay the crosshairs on it and shoot, what sport in that?"; he'd taken the scope off and now only open sights and his eye), and out of the corner of his eye he saw his brother and the old hired man watching. He rested the stock firmly, very firmly in his shoulder, settled the rifle on the distant bird, so far it blurred and nothing but the whole bird to sight at, it so small it filled the entire sight. And shot.

Profound change. Profoundist. Down it dropped. Plummeted. Straight down. He could hear it hit.

"Good thing you didn't make a hole in the silo roof," his brother muttered, but obviously impressed.

He went in through the wooden gate, the whining dog going wild, the dog seized the first pigeon, although the dog was so fat and used to cooked scraps of steak and pork chops it never ate more than the head or a piece of pigeon breast, whichever the bullet made a hole into.

Leonard inspected the birds one by one, and this is what still made him shake a little, just a little, the inspection afterwards that he did not need to do, but always forced himself to do, remembering each time he did so his not wanting to shoot things when he was very young and being ordered to by his father when he was twelve or so, the first time, and how his father had put the rifle in his hand, another rifle then, assuredly, and had chosen a random bird, just to have him shoot something, a woodpecker, a bird he'd always liked, a woodpecker! and he had shot and hit it. The bird had come down, alarming him, horrifying him, yet in the fatherly approval that he desired delighting him too. He had not looked at the bird, could not, but ever after that he had, always examined that which he had brought to death, picked up the bundle of feathers, felt for the point of being hit, and ever amazed at the awful impact of the bullet. That was it, really, the real heart and matter of it, he thought, even as he fed the slender gray little bullets into the clip, nosed them in, the brass case seated firmly, and felt the bullets, so tiny, a quarter the size of his little finger, and from that what awful impact! What terrible change from something so small, hardly to be believed, and sometimes he had mused on whether one bullet, so little, so few grams there, whether one could hurt *him*, whether if he shot himself somewhere, arm, foot or wherever, if it would hurt. And knew it would, smiled at the thought, shot a hog for butchering once; and was astounded at how the 260-pound lumbering beast had thundered down as if a cosmic scythe had struck with whirlwind force to reap off its legs, it had scuttled down so suddenly. With awful impact the bullet found home. The turning bullet goes home (and why "home"? he asked, why that word?), the flesh is pounded to jelly, the bones that the victim thinks will surely last a thousand years are riddled and smashed (he had felt the crunched crispness like rattled potato chips of the bones of pheasants he had shot) . But the bullet carries its own palliation, he thought grimly. It was said that the bullet deadens all pain in the locale of striking. Perhaps that was why the dying animals offered yet to flee from him instead of from that which was killing them—the bullet within.

He crossed the fence, driving the dog back for sure this time, went down along the pasture, picked up a stray cat at forty yards, scrubbing along the fence row, tacky and mean, and shot it dead. The cat went straight into the air, wrestling with something there, and down again, thrashed along for ten feet or so. When Leonard came up, it lay on its side, hissing and stroking with one forepaw, the other side paralyzed apparently, a smoking and open wound in its belly.

"What's your history, cat?" he asked, touched it with the rifle muzzle to see if it would need a new bullet. It did not move at the gesture. "Only one life today?" he asked. And thought, god, god, profoundly altered, changed, eternally for it, eternally changed by that awful meeting of something brought crushing and unexpected through space to meet it here, unexpected and unpredestined except as the shooter destines, now in one casual determination. He watched, pulling at the hurting bandage on his neck. Hissing of remarkable anger, a rage, that changed to a terrible rattle in its throat and two great spasms, and freezing in that clenched posture. Forever, forever, Leonard thought; or as long as the bugs will let it alone—that's how long this forever is.

There was a tightness around his forehead, a coolness in his chest; it always came upon him when he watched something die, this meditative and hurting helplessness at the irreversibility of it, even if he had brought it, but the bringing had been from a distance, the dying was up close. This nearness of the smashing, the impact, irreversible, irretrievable. He felt it more powerfully now. Especially now.

Smooth barrel, oiled stock, smooth, easy, he walked. The nervous cattle lifted their beautiful heads, pointed their tipped white ears and muzzles and looked at him. He remembered vaguely Homer and the lines of "cow-eyed"; was it cow-eyed dawn or cow-eyed Diana? Large, brown, beautiful eyes of these animals; immense eyelashes; Homer was right. The cattle sniffed, backed away, ran a little. He worked through them, crossed the creek. The cattle circled, some went ahead, some behind, and that was strange, he thought, for he expected them to go on to the other end of the pasture as they always had done, far away from the farm buildings, but today they did not, hung close, sniffing with that heavy challenging but frightened way and then running a little, circling, and coming back to study him.

Leonard walked along the edge of the creek, the creek itself about forty feet wide in that area, but the water at its bottom only six inches deep and two feet wide, a nice creek with minnows and frogs in abundance. The grass was tall already, pale green and heavy with occasional giant burdocks lifted like watchers. Some of the cattle went ahead of him, splashed through the mud and up the slippery far bank where he would follow. Most of the bank was too steep to be crossed at all, the straight slice of black dirt, caved off in chunks at intervals, and down there the ribbon of water in the sand, the curling motion. He looked for raccoons, knew he would see none now, and remembered, not so certain, how he had seen one in broad daylight up on the farm one spring, and watched, looked at the placid water reflecting reeds, the smear of sky, himself.

Four weeks before he had come (he and his wife) to visit his mother; in the best of health, he thought, except for that persistent new back ache, something clamped on him that wouldn't let go, and he'd lost weight, everyone noticed that right away, and he'd said it was his diet, one that had never worked before, some slight fevers, dizziness. And now confirmed in the ancient certainty of his own mortality, yes truly that over the easy optimism of the others—oh if you find it soon enough they can get it, can work miracles, great doctors nowadays, and so on—but he knew the statistics on this one, most assuredly, two years or three. In three weeks, in a moment really after that first biopsy, from healthy man to dying man. He had not thought of death, before, coming to him, no healthy person of thirty-three would except perhaps melodramatically when having flu or a cold or driving a car fast. He had thought much on it these last three weeks.

He went through the grove of willows, young trees near the creek bed. He was tired now, but he told himself he would not be, not yet. He was though, as he had told himself the cancer could not spread, but it had. He could feel the cut on his neck burning, and the cold lump in him on his side. The young green grass there on the other side of the creek was very heavy, and he looked down at his shoes, hearing as if for eternity the shuff with each step of the grass—shuff, shuff, shuff, not watchful now, knowing he was drifting, bitter and drifting.

The jackrabbit took him by surprise, gave him that sudden striking jolt in his heart region, the flash and movement. The big rabbit had fled the brush, bounded easily up past the spring there on the pasture hillside, a big old jackrabbit, gray with age and remnant of winter coat. Leonard waited, trailing it with the points of the rifle sights. When the animal stopped, as he thought it might, dropped to a pause, let its tall ears fall over its back, Leonard shot it, a good long shot. The rabbit gave a spasm and frantically kicked in a circle when it hit the ground again. Leonard was in no rush getting there. The rabbit was dead, of course, head covered with dust, the dead film on the eyes already. Knobbed feet, old powerful legs, blistered haunches. Tiny bullet, smallest penetration not even to be found but by someone who knew, a fragment of weight against the big heavy rabbit, really a miracle of sorts.

"You were an old one," Leonard said. "You should have been prepared, shouldn't you?" touching it with the rifle tip. "How many near misses from coyote or fox or rifle have you had?" He reloaded the clip and grinned. I cannot miss today, he thought. Everything comes down today.

He went down the hill, breathing hard, his head aching a little now, his neck itching. The doctors had encouraged exercise but not too much, to keep his strength, the way the doctors always could blandly respond in clichés, yes one needs milk and exercise and sunshine. For what should he keep his strength, and he knew, for those days of debility that awaited him, this debilitating disease that would grind him down to an emaciated parody of himself until he contracted something like pneumonia that would kill him. Build strength for that.

The cattle at the pinch of the pasture along the creek did not go on ahead of him, as they would before, but turned and came back, right around him.

"Something scares you more than I do," he murmured.

There was brush and trees along the creek there. A blackbird, the redwing fighter came to heckle him, right over his head, squawking fiercely, and he thought of shooting, decided against it for no good reason. The bird drifted back, apparently keeping near its ground nest, and another little bird came to whistle and shriek at him, a tiny bird, a wren he believed, tiny and brown and very beautiful; he had seen the kind up by the farm. The bird fluttered away, across the creek and to a cottonwood tree quite a distance from him, and he, feeling daring at the chance because of his shooting well that day, balanced the rifle on his left hand, fastened it tightly with his right, and feeling absolutely nothing at all at that distance, shot. There was an astonishing puff of feathers and it came down.

At that moment too he sensed rather than saw a motion, and there through the brush, on the other side of the creek, not fifty feet away, was a car parked, and he saw in the clearing a little distance from the car the figure come up, and he knew suddenly why the cattle would not come any further, this alien thing blocking their way.

There was a motion of the figure as if reaching for something, groping wildly for something, the person had been asleep, Leonard could tell that, and startled with suddenness, and now blinking, staring around, and coming in his alarmed awakening at last to a position on his hands and knees on the blanket behind the car, he at last seeing Leonard and from the drifting feathers, what Leonard shot at—and hit.

He stared like one engulfed, sprung there in his strange posture, caught absolutely, the astonished face, the disheveled hair, the impotent look in the eyes, and the outrage on the face at being caught thus, impotent. For he, Leonard, had the gun.

Leonard knew in that instant that this was the man who was wanted, this was the killer, putting it all together, the necessity of having to take down the fence to park here, the isolated location, the mid-afternoon sleep, and the fright of the young man. He wondered if there was another or two or three. He could see nothing, no one in the car or along the creek.

"Shooting birds, hunh?" the young man over there said, his voice choking. "That was quite a shot." He knelt, leaning forward on his hands, crouched like a dog, really, looking at Leonard, and Leonard realized then that the other was waiting too, trying to determine Leonard's exact purpose there, whether he was caught. "You handle a gun pretty good."

"Not as good as some others," Leonard said. "Are you alone here?"

"Oh sure, just me." He tried a grin. "Came down for a break; such a nice peaceful spot."

He was twenty or twenty-one, Leonard guessed, although he found it difficult to give precise ages, always had, a young man with a decent face, slender, a hundred and fifty pounds or so, five feet eight he guessed, medium brown hair, dark blue eyes, a sort of sandy and freckled look, and he, Leonard, trying to see the mark of a killer on that face, could see nothing, realizing once again that you could not tell anything from the face of a person, nothing at all, from the eyes perhaps, but from the face, nothing, no more than you could tell the character of a cow by the hair on its ears.

"This is your land, I guess?" he asked.

"My brother's," Leonard said.

"I don't suppose he'd like me taking down the gate and driving here in the pasture?"

"No, I don't suppose he would," Leonard said.

"Well you know I saw the lane coming down here and the trees and I just figured there was a crick along here. I remembered how nice it was to stop and rest beside a stream like this when I was a kid and my old man and I went up to Minnesota, and I just couldn't resist it. No damage done."

Leonard said nothing. He studied the car, a Chevrolet about ten years old, with a '71 Iowa license. That would be O'Brien County, he thought, remembering that trivia from his high school days. "You from up around Sheldon?" he asked.

The other's face tightened a little. He was turning wary. "Sure am," he said after a moment. "Sibley."

"We used to play Sibley in football. In my time."

"Still do, I guess. I never played football. Played baseball a little."

"Maybe you know my younger brother. He's about your age. Played baseball too." Knowing somehow that the other had not played baseball either.

"Oh I never played much," he said. "Might have seen him though."

Leonard thought of it, the young man from Sibley, wiped out the family not ten miles away, hardly possible. Always the serious evil should come from farther away than Sibley, from Chicago or Memphis or some other such distant place; oh, he knew well enough of the petty offenses, chicken or hay thieves who were either young punks or the old town derelicts, but he could scarcely accept the possibility that anyone who could commit serious and terrible offense could be someone truly close, a neighbor almost, a person from his own state, so near they were almost known to each other. Somberly he remembered that the penitentiary at Fort Madson was filled with good young men of his native state.

The young man fidgeted, squatting there on his haunches. "Yeh,

I sure enjoyed that snooze. Tell your brother thanks." He found a pack of cigarettes, took out a bent one. "I'll get out of here soon's I finish a cigarette. Wake me up you know." He looked at Leonard. "Care for one?" he asked, rising and coming to the side of the creek. The young man moved easily, nothing strange, nothing warped about him. "Pretty steep bank along here."

The young man put a stone in the cigarette pack and threw it across, the pack landing near Leonard's feet. He went to it carefully, keeping his eye on the other, not turning his back on him. He got the pack and holding his rifle with pretended carelessness, the tip pointing about ten feet to the left of the young man's head, he lit the one cigarette.

"Last one, huh?"

"Oh there's more in the car," the young man said, starting that way.

"No, don't go," Leonard said with sudden sharpness, his hand automatically fastening hard on the stock of the rifle.

The other looked at him, turning back calmly. It was then that Leonard saw the blotches on the other's pant leg, dark, almost the color of an oil stain or old blood. The other saw him looking, noticed it too, and when he sat down he kept the leg behind him. "You just give the word if you want another cigarette," he said.

"Sure," Leonard said.

"Got a bandage, I see," the other said, pointing at his own neck to where the bandage was on Leonard's.

"A little operation I had just a little while ago," Leonard said.

"What for? You know, I had an operation once, but that was some years ago, when I was a kid. Mastoid operation. Oh, that was tough. The nurse went away, and I pulled everything out. Could have died, I guess. What's yours for?"

"A biopsy to see if I have cancer."

"Cancer." Ah, what a word, Leonard thought, almost smiling,

a word that carries its own exclamation point after it. "How'd it turn out?"

"I have cancer."

"Son of a bitch," the young man said with a kind of understanding and sympathy that Leonard would not have believed possible.

"Now I do a little shooting to take my mind off it," he said, knowing that his mind had not been taken off it since he found out.

"If all your shots are like that last one, you're some hell of a shot."

"Do you do any shooting?"

The blue eyes came up, studied him a moment. "Me? No. Oh, I've hunted now and then."

"What do you hunt?" Yes, what do you give palliation to, was it palliation the five in the farmhouse wanted yesterday afternoon?

"You know, rabbits, pheasant. The best ones are out of season, ain't they?"

Somehow shaping them together, Leonard thought, he knowing that anything he shot here in May was out of season, from pigeons to rabbits to song birds. Just as people were out of season.

"You ever been to Craig?"

There was a careful hesitation. "Craig? Is that a town? No, I don't believe I've been there. No."

"Some people were murdered there yesterday. Farmhouse right near Craig."

"Is that right?"

"Nobody can figure out why the young hired man was shot too." Leonard waited. The other pulled at grass stems, acted as if he had not heard. "He was a young fellow about your age. Shot with the family; weren't even relatives."

The blue eyes looked at him. "I hadn't heard about it. I wasn't listening to the news. I bet it makes quite a story around these parts."

"Yes, it's quite a story all right," Leonard said.

A story of choosing, he thought, the kind of choosing that had troubled him in these last few weeks. He had been chosen like the five in the house by Craig, like he had chosen the squirrel or the cat to shoot. God had nothing to do with it really, he thought—there was no evidence of such involvement one way or the other—but yet it remained that something somewhere, inside him or out, had chosen him. By strange accident perhaps. His being somewhere or not being somewhere, perhaps—as that young hired man's bad luck to be at the house where the murderer struck—had made the difference. He was not aware of any commission of awful sin to warrant his death at thirty-six, or whenever. No, it was best to leave God out of it, until we knew ourselves better, and that would take a thousand years at least.

An icy chill at his abdomen, snuff and crawl of cancerous lumps, like cool rats in his belly.

"I wonder," he said, clearing his throat, "if the motive was robbery." The other said nothing, picked at the grass by handfuls.

But what could I be robbed of? Leonard asked himself. Could anything really be so anxious to get his flesh?

"Or maybe it was a whim."

"A what?" the other said.

"You know, just a hell of it, spur of the moment thing. Just to kill something. The way you shoot things sometimes, like birds."

"Yeh. Like birds you can't even eat," in a petulant tone. Vaguely accusatory, alluding to his shot of the wren, Leonard knew. He could have laughed at that.

"Or maybe an old hatred. An old score to be settled."

The other grunted something, dug at the grass and weeds with his slender hands.

What offense had he given to his body at some distant time or place, what had he defiled, and it had lain in wait, remembering?

Something tiny, that is not wanted, doesn't belong there, something driven apart, and then it returns, burrows into one cell, blasts it apart, enjoys it, it's wonderful, tries another and another, loves the way they're ripped and bloody, devours them, destroys them, expands them till they crack. Ah!

"Or perhaps just crazy . . ."

The other started at the words, turned rigid. Leonard from his side feeling the jolt here of meeting something lethal. The other's hand still snatching at the dirt.

". . . just madness. Somebody went crazy, came upon them, killed them . . ."

The other flung the handful of dirt and grass to the side. "Crazy?" he screamed at Leonard. "They don't have to be crazy."

Very calmly Leonard sat, watched the other. "Oh, what else then?" he said. "What else to account for it?" He cranked his neck against the bite beneath the bandage. And what else to account for the rampant surge of inflamed and maddened cells within him? What else?

"I don't know," the other said, quieter, his voice still high-pitched. "Don't have to be crazy though," he added doggedly.

"No, I don't suppose so," Leonard said. Thinking, what enormous pride we all have, accepting guilt for anything but our insanity.

He considered laying the gun on him then, saying he knew who he was, or better yet working it out of him, under threat of the rifle having him confess, yes that would be better. "All right you, the game is up. You murdered that family by Craig, didn't you?" And he looked across that small distance, judging it expertly, thinking how easy it would be to shoot at that distance, separated by the gulf of the steep-banked creek, he looking now with clinical detachment at the sandy complexion, the round mouth sucking the cigarette, the slender wiry body, he considered it coldly, even as his left hand pulled at the itching biting cut on his neck, yes it would be easy, no need to even get a confession, no need to even approach the body after the shot, except perhaps to see where the bullet entered, it would be easy to nail this creature, simple, no more than a routine palliation, no worse than shooting that cat or the wren.

The other sat up straight, lifted his left hand to him. "Something the matter?" he asked. "What you looking like that for?"

"What?" Leonard said. The other was frightened, really frightened.

"I mean we're just talking, having a cigarette. I'll move the car, get out of here, if that's what you want, sorry about coming in here. Should have got out right away, I guess. Dumb of me to sit here smoking a cigarette."

How do I look, Leonard wondered, noted the point of the rifle had dropped, nosed in the direction of the other one, pointing at him, and he staring at the young man.

He tried a laugh. "Just thinking to myself," he said. "Whenever I think about this cancer I get that way. Can't help it." He pulled the rifle erect again.

He had had a dream, repeated more than once, of himself in a foreign city (was it Leipzig, was it the terrible experience locked in the brain of a forebear of a century and a half before, passed on to him? five generations of nightmare) and there in late afternoon beside a stone church, the narrow streets cobbled to the church side, a figure leaned in a niche of the church (echoes of war around them), leaned there as if to make himself unseen, the figure in uniform, straggler, still the tatters of blue and red of the cloth, blood turned black on his wrapped head, with that measureless weariness on him, and the round eyes watching him. He (Leonard, whoever he was in the dream) came closer and the tired eyes of the beaten man fastened on him, watching him, and in his own hands (or in the hands of someone just in front of him that he was following, he could not be sure) was a club and he raised it and with a sudden thrusting powerful energy he struck at the head of the soldier, smashed the blood-ridden head, heard the dreadful sound like an axe dull on a soft stump.

A century and a half since Leipzig. Yes, he could do it, he could kill the young man, without pretense of compassion, confession, anything, just kill him, and told himself it was ridiculous, absurd, he who had never contemplated murder of anyone in thirty-odd years, and even as he thought it he studied the motion of the other stooping to fold the blanket, the fright of the other, this absurd fear of him, Leonard, that made him even more willing to do it, now contemplated a neat mark on the other to put his bull's-eye on. He would feel nothing. Neither of them would feel anything.

At the same time he could have laughed. Was it possible? he asked, possible that a murderer of a whole family and hired man to boot would be frightened of him? No one had been afraid of him before, no need to be. And here the young man was obviously scared. It was amazing to him. He wanted to discuss it with the young man, but what could he say, how could he begin? "Say, are you afraid of me?" Pointing the rifle at him perhaps? As he might have asked the terrified cat a while before. The rifle made one invincible.

"Well, I got to be getting on," the other said with his folded blanket under his arm, standing there facing Leonard as if asking permission to go to the car.

"Yes. Be sure and close the fence gate good and tight. These are young calves in here and pretty wild."

"Sure will. I know all about fences." The other went on then, to the car, got in. Leonard went the few feet so that he was opposite to him, so he could watch. The old car's engine cranked over, finally started with a clatter, and the machine backed away. The young man stopped at the fence, carefully put up the wires, looking down through the trees to where Leonard stood, obscured he knew, watching. How easy it would be, the press, the snap of sound, the awful impact. He stood there, chilled, feeling the cold pressure of relentless and terrible things growing within him, feeling the stinging bite of his neck as if a snake had toothed him there.

The wires were painstakingly finished, the young man drove on, out of sight immediately but Leonard able to hear the retreat of sound.

All the way back to the farmhouse he shot anything that moved, two cottontails, a big brown thrasher, one crow, and a woodpecker. He did not miss.

Old Schwier

Rudolph Schwier was the richest man in Charleston. He lived on the hill at the east end of town, up away from the river, in a shabby old frame house that had been white once but was turning gray. A house never made money for anybody, he always said. That's what he told the wives of his farm tenants whenever they would timidly suggest wallpaper or calcimine for their chicken-coop houses. Old Schwier owned thirty-one farms, spread around Charleston in all directions, even across the river in South Dakota. He owned the creamery and one of the town's two grain elevators, too.

Schwier had come to Charleston from Schleswig-Holstein when he was seventeen. He worked for a year as a hired hand for a bachelor, whose name no one remembered anymore, on a farm northeast of town until one day the bachelor got kicked in the head by a horse and was killed. Schwier brought him to town in a buckboard and they buried him. Schwier kept on farming out there and it wasn't long before it was called the Schwier place. He was a hard-working man, no one could deny that; before he was twenty-five, he had two other quarter sections. Even then no one liked him much. The farmers around, who were far from gentle themselves, said he was a brute with his horses and cows, and besides that they could never talk to Schwier; he had nothing to say to them, and if they paused and leaned over the fence to await his coming to the end of the corn row at cultivating time, Schwier would simply turn his team and head back and not even look up at them.

When he was a little past thirty he married the fat daughter of one of his tenants. She turned into a stolid and heavy and silent woman and her arms were always burdened with kids. Schwier had four girls and six boys and when each was old enough, eight or so, they were working twelve and fourteen hours a day, just as he was. They went to school when Schwier found time to let them go, and they were all plodding and thick-witted and ham-fisted and they were supposed to be stupid. They got away one by one, hitchhiking out or catching the train or getting married and leaving if they could. If it was one of the boys who left, Schwier would go into an enormous rage. He got his buggy and a boy or two and the blacksnake whip and he drove around the countryside, asking all the farmers if they had seen his son. The only one he ever caught was the oldest; he found him under a wooden culvert and old Schwier pulled him out of there and tied a rope around the boy's waist and dragged him home. He took the boy out into the barn and beat him half the night. The boy went around with a cringing look and with a crouched back and he shambled after that, but he tried again within six months. This time he was not caught.

The tenth and last of the Schwiers was Diedrich. He was born when his mother was nearly forty-five. There was trouble and Schwier was off to a sale and it was the dead of winter and by the time the daughter got back with the neighbor woman the woman was dead and the boy was on the floor beside her, bawling up through the blood and water and slimy filament. Diedrich was a frail boy. He was raised by his sister, Bertha—she was eleven years older than him. Perhaps because of the boy, she stayed longer than most, until he was nine. Schwier got a hired girl then to take care of things, and when she, too, ran away, Schwier was furious, because he had been paying her money. He hitched up his team of bays to the buggy and he yelled at Diedrich to open the gate. The boy couldn't get it open quickly enough and the high-spirited animals were whipped over him and the buggy went over his legs. Both legs were broken in four places. The boy crawled back to the house. Old Schwier tried to set his legs when he got back, without the girl. The pain was terrible and the boy howled day and night even when under the threat of the whip, and after three days Old Schwier took him to town to see a doctor. The doctor broke his legs again and reset them, but it was no use. He was always crippled.

He managed to walk a little after a year, and eventually he could discard the crutches and canes, but the walking was always laborious and shambling. Old Schwier made fun of his son when he saw him walking and he would laugh and copy the boy's steps.

"Walk right, young fool," he shouted, laughing. "Walk so." And he tapped the young boy on the breast. "At least you won't leave, will you, ah?"

When the Depression came, Schwier dug up some of the money he'd hoarded—he had never trusted banks—and he bought the bankrupt creamery, and then he moved to town. He bought the house on the hill and a brand new 1932 Packard. It was a gigantic car, and it was the only new car sold in Charleston that year. Old Schwier didn't want anyone to know he couldn't drive a car, since he had never had one, so he sent Diedrich crippling down the hill to the Packard garage to take lessons, and after that the son was Old Schwier's chauffeur. The old man always sat in the backseat when they drove; they never drove far, usually only out to a tenant's place to see how things were going, or to Sioux City to a whorehouse.

The town began to see Old Schwier then as the farmers always had. The townspeople could never before believe the farmers, who were always complaining about something. But they, too, found that he was cold and tyrannical and mean. He finagled his way into the feed mill and within a year he owned it all. He had too much money to distrust banks and he was named a director of the Charleston Savings Bank. The foreclosures increased, rates went up, and when Old Schwier got through, his bank was the only one in town. They whispered about him, and the low-paid men cursed him and made vague threats, but that was all they could do. Old Schwier employed almost half of Charleston.

When he came downtown in the Packard he would be dressed in overalls and the buttons at the side would be unbuttoned, and sometimes the fly, too, and he would walk down to the bank. He chewed tobacco and would spit on the sidewalk and on the bank floor or wherever it was convenient. Everyone hated Old Schwier, but everyone was also timid.

Old Schwier always liked his hair cropped short, in a crisp, Kraut style, as everyone in town said, and when Old Schwier walked in, the barber would hurry with the man he was working on so Schwier would not have to wait too long. He held the mortgage on the barbershop, too.

Diedrich would never get out of the car on those weekly trips from the hill to the bank or to the barbershop. He sat behind the wheel and said nothing and did nothing, even when the weather was hot and the sun was full on him. Only the black eyes in his face would ever move much, and they hardly ever at all.

They were an odd pair, the town decided. The town hated and feared them both. They hated the father because he was rich and powerful and ruthless, and the son they hated because he was his father's servant.

The talk was always of wickedness and scandal concerning Old Schwier. Everyone hated him and avoided him if they could and they talked of him, unless he was there among them and then they fell silent. A young new Lutheran minister went up to the house on the hill one afternoon to carry his missionary zeal to the root of the evil of the town, and he got thrown out bodily by the fierce and wicked old man. The minister walked around with a cane for a few weeks after that, and he preached against evil from the pulpit, and he prayed openly for Old Schwier's soul.

When Schwier heard about it he spat a glob on the sidewalk and laughed.

The war came and went and nothing changed with the old man and the son. The house grew more shabby, but there was always a Prussian cleanliness and neatness about the yard and the porch and as much as one could see of the inside of the house itself—Old Schwier saw to it that the housekeeper took care of that. There was still the 1932 Packard, immaculate and polished on the outside, but a garage man reported once he had seen the interior of the backseat where Old Schwier always sat, and the floor was covered with the slime of the old man's spitting. Old Schwier did not change, he was still erect and although there were lines on his face he did not look older. His hair was still a cropped steel-gray and his eyes were a cold metallic color. Old Schwier was always the same, and the new generation came to fear and hate him as much as the old. Only Diedrich had changed; his back had bent, his face was old, his mouth was hard and dry and lipless and there were wrinkles on his thin, cold face. Some said he looked older than his father.

The first attack came very suddenly. Old Schwier and Diedrich had driven out to one of the farms south of town and Old Schwier was walking through the hog yard with the farmer and Diedrich was hobbling after them when Old Schwier gave a kind of howl and he fell and lay writhing in the manure. There was spittle around his chin when they pulled him up and he was clutching his chest.

"Stand up," Diedrich hissed. "Stand up."

The old man tried to stand and he could not and he clutched at the two of them and his eyes were dumb and terrified.

They got him back to the house and the doctor came out right away. It was a heart attack.

They took Schwier back to town in the Packard and put him in the house up on the hill. No one saw him for more than a month. When they did see him again, he had changed; his face had lost the German ruddiness, he was a ghostly gray color now, and his hands shook. When he got out of the car he walked very slowly and heavily and at the sidewalk it came on him again and he fell and had to call for help. A couple of passing boys stopped to help him up the few steps into the bank. It was like looking death in the face, one of the boys said afterwards, to look at Old Schwier. The old man was very frightened. Diedrich did not get out of the car at all.

Old Schwier had never had use for a doctor, but there was one out almost every day now. They told him he was old, he had a murmur and it looked bad. No, there was nothing they could do really. They would try, of course, to help, and to ease any pain.

Old Schwier spent the summer sitting in a rocking chair on the front porch. He had no breath left and he could hardly walk without Diedrich to help him. He had stopped chewing tobacco and his voice was very soft now. The bankers and the doctors came up the hill to see him now. The town was glad to miss Old Schwier. It served the old son of a bitch right, they said.

After the third heart attack that fall, Schwier had to stay in bed for nearly a month. When he arose again there was a visible tremor not only in his hands but in his entire body. Even his head shook now, slightly and perpetually. He was frail and he looked his full seventy-eight.

When he recovered enough to move again he had Diedrich drive him down to the minister's house. They were there together, he and the minister, for over an hour, and when Old Schwier came out again he was weeping.

The minister made daily visitations to the house on the hill. He brought his little case along and there was the sacrament of communion there often.

The changes were many then. The old man wept and prayed most of the day, and he called Diedrich in and wanted him to pray, too, but Diedrich only looked at him and hobbled out again.

"I have sinned so much," the old man wailed. He said he wanted his son to forgive him and for them to love each other. Old Schwier had the minister contact the Red Cross to try and locate his children but the Red Cross could not find any of them. They had probably all changed their names, the minister said.

Old Schwier threw out the housemaid he'd had and he got an elderly woman to do his cooking and cleaning. He took $40,000 and had an organ installed in the church and had a small gold plaque, "In memory of my beloved wife, Hilda," placed on it. He went to church every Sunday then, and the minister seated him in the front pew and delivered several sermons in succession to God's forgiveness and love. Schwier sold a couple of farms and gave the money to the church towards a new one they would build in the spring. It was a gift from God, the minister said. There was talk that even the president of the synod would be there to help with the cornerstone. Other things changed, too. Old Schwier lowered the rent on his farms, he sent out fence material and paint and wallpaper without being asked. He had the minister say public prayers for himself and his wife and his children.

I have done such terrible things, he told the minister. I have sinned so terribly. They called Diedrich in and asked about his legs and if he wanted to go to Rochester to the Mayo Clinic to be helped, and Old Schwier said he would spend anything to help his son. Bless you, my child, he said, with love in his eyes, bless you for being with me even when I was terrible and cruel. Diedrich, who had lately taken to chewing tobacco, only spat on the floor.

When they rarely went downtown, Old Schwier tried to be benevolent and kind. He took candy and small coins with him to press on the children he saw. Everyone said he was a wonderful old man. They said he had made a mistake and he knew it and he was really fine now. Only the old-timers would sometimes recall the old Old Schwier, but they were shushed.

In the spring the church was begun with the president of the synod there and Schwier standing between the minister and the president, the old man leaning heavily on two canes. It was to be the most beautiful church in the area, the president said. A month later Schwier sold a couple more farms and gave the money to the school for a new gymnasium. It was to be called Schwier Auditorium over the protests of the generous old man. The Sioux City papers, covering the event, called him a benefactor and philanthropist.

Old Schwier gave to the hospital too, and he felt badly that he could not help more, but the town had already built a new one just after the war.

Gradually he forgot and the town forgot and he was loved and adulated and his kindness was known and his smile was common. Only with the minister did he still sometimes weep and be concerned.

"Has my God forgiven me?" he asked.

"Yes, God can forgive any sin."

"And my wickedness, too?"

"Yes, and any wickedness—God loves you."

"Will he take me to Himself?" Schwier asked. He had heard much of the church's words, as "wickedness" and "to Himself," and could repeat them.

"If you have fully repented," the minister said.

"I do repent. I do love, and I feel His love."

"Then He will take you."

The time came in the fall. There were three heart attacks in rapid succession and the doctors came and the ministers, too. They did everything they could for him. The minister gave him the last communion, which Old Schwier understood. His mind was clear, the minister said, his sins were washed away. Afterwards Old Schwier called for Diedrich and he had the son read the will. Much went to charity and to the church but the bulk of the large estate went to the children, and Diedrich was to search for the others and if they could not be found within five years, he was to have it all.

"My son," Old Schwier said when Diedrich had finished reading the will, "come and I will give you my last blessing."

"You have no right to bless anyone," Diedrich said.

"My sins are forgiven. I have repented. I am ready to see my God."

"You will never see any God."

"My poor child. You don't believe. But I believe and I am at rest and happy. Come, let us pray together now. I know we cannot be together long."

"We have never been together."

"We can be now. My God has forgiven me my sins."

"What kind of a God is that?"

"What do you mean?"

"A God that let you do what you have done and then let you by because you change your mind at the very last minute."

"I have seen my error."

"No one could forgive you."

"Everyone has forgiven. The people who hated me love me now."

"Only because you have money."

"God has forgiven me."

"How do you know?"

"Because I believe."

"And I believe he has not. He is not so easily fooled as the stupid people of this town."

"But he has, don't you see? I have repented, and he has forgiven me."

"I haven't forgiven you, father, and neither have any of my brothers and sisters. We will never forgive you."

"Oh, oh, oh," the father wailed, and the tears ran down his ashen, lined cheeks.

"How can God forgive you if we do not? What kind of a God is that?" Diedrich almost smiled then.

"I believe. I do believe. He has forgiven."

"Then we should all do what you have done and wait until God, if there is such a thing, comes to us out of the sky."

"Don't test me now, not now."

"You could not live long enough to be forgiven, father. Forgiveness cannot come in the last second of eighty evil years."

"There is no hope then . . ."

"For you there isn't."

"Get away from me. Get away."

"Are you getting angry now, father? Anger may kill you."

"I want to see the reverend. Let me see him."

"Your sins are forgiven, you said."

"They are. They are all washed away. I believe. I believe. I have repented."

"Then why do you want to see the reverend? Are you still doubtful? Are you worried?"

"No! I know my God wants me. He loves me."

"Good. Then die, father, before he remembers all you have done and changes his fickle mind."

"You devil!" the father cried. "Go, you devil!"

"In a moment. I have much time."

"I do not bless you. I take it back. Goddamn you!" The father sat bolt upright, shrieking and panting, his voice strained and loud. "Goddamn!" His eyes bulged, his face flushed scarlet and became ashen, and his voice choked on his scarlet phlegm. "Goddamn!" His voice weakened, and the door opened and the others came in, the doctors and the minister. "God . . . God . . . God." Old Schwier choked and he reeled, staring at a place above Diedrich's head. They caught him then and the needles came out, but it was too late. Old Rudolph Schwier was dead.

"He was crying 'God, God!'" one of the doctors said, his voice hushed and a little awed.

"It's as if he had seen Him," the minister said. "He died seeing the God of his forgiveness."

"Yes," Diedrich said quietly, folding his hands when the minister began to pray.

Anniversary

Two years to the day, McDonald thought, two years since he had last come through Lincoln, Nebraska, in the dead of winter, going west to see his relatives during the Christmas let-out. Through the begrimed train window he saw the wood frame houses emerge frigidly from the somnolent snow-blown land, and the trees, like exposed fretful nerves, black against the gray December sky. He vaguely remembered the curve of the railroad track and the landscape from that time two years before, but now everything was very clear to him, chiseled there, as if he saw it all for the first time really, as if perhaps his eyes had altered in those two years. And still he felt an eagerness akin to that rush of the time before. There had been the quivering warmth in his body, the specific need, the hurry to get off the train, the push through the clusters of people to see her there, for they had written regularly and impassionedly that first fall. His face colored a little, the prickles of heat he felt were like a mirror to him, as he remembered those letters, the heart yearnings of a newly lonely man who had imagined that he had drunk deeply of unloneliness. And she, Wanda, replying, matched his passion almost word for word (a part of him thought coolly of her at the time and wondered at that, and he had ascribed her parrotings of feeling to her lack of training in communication). McDonald smiled again, thinking of that misjudgment, he who had once thought he knew all of mankind, he, James R. McDonald, assistant professor of English at the University of Missouri, teacher of literature (Truth, Life, Humanity), and of composition.

Six years before, he had come from the Air Force—two pleasant years as an officer at a base in England—armed with his GI bill and, as he now reflected, an empty-headedness, and made his way to the M.A. in one year in the company of ascetics. He, as those others apparently did not, had that perpetual yearning, that perpetual need of a woman, the impelling desire and want, for he was in his early twenties, in the prime of his life, and those two easy years in England had only confirmed his hunger. He had seen associates wed through the same desperation to have a woman (so confessed to him by the grooms in stolid puzzlement over beer glasses a few months following weddings), while he went sardonically and dilatorily on dates with birdy female graduate students—unsexed bodies like storewindow dummies and faces like parakeet beaks—evenings stiff with conversation and milked-out culture and the heady pronouncements of likes, dislikes, and logic, dredged from a convenient book or lecture, and nothing else, while his producing gonads cried to heaven for aid. In the coffeerooms the younger, married professors, affecting crew-cuts and virility, clucked approvingly over the vibrance of Dylan Thomas's insanities, and sniggered with admiration at the dynamic sex allusions of the visiting literati; they huddled together in closet-like rooms like frigid children before a fireplace to simper at fleshy jokes told by transient linguists. They giggled over Chaucer, and vibrated over Fielding, and snickered over D. H . Lawrence, and perspired over John Updike (that Rabbit man); and the fairies in the department looked him over and approached in sly, nuzzling, knee-touching familiarity and retreated before his somber stare.

He met Wanda Overson the summer he began work on his Ph.D. On a hot, bad night in July he had driven down to the road-houses along the highway where there were unnerving attempts at jazz offered up by college students, and he saw her, a woman a little older than most of the others there, slender, fairly tall, hard smooth legs, and with black hair and dark eyes. They danced; she said she liked the way he danced, and they arranged to see each other again.

She was twenty-nine, a divorcee, with a boy nine years old—that first night he went to her house the child came up to him and shook hands, man-like, a frail boy, skinny, pale, with dark, deep-socketed eyes as if blackened by blows; he said his name was Trevor—and McDonald smiled carefully and affectedly at the boy, knowing this would please the mother. She did like that, talked about it in the car on the way to dinner that night, how kind he was, saying too that Trevor meant more to her than anything else in the world—her whole life was just lived for her son—and she would like anybody who treated her son well. She liked kindness, she said, she liked to be treated nice, that made more difference to her than anything else, money or anything. Of course she liked nice things too; she really had the tastes of a lady, she said, even if she was only a secretary. She had gone with a few very wealthy men, she said, lifting her eyes to look carefully at him, but of course none had meant a thing to her. She had gone with the owner of a ladies shoe store who had wanted to marry her, but his father who had the money didn't like it, wanted him to marry a rich girl who wasn't a divorcee, but she could have had him any time she wanted him, she said with a faint curl of upper lip. And there had been her boss, ex-boss rather, old Mr. Curtis who owned and managed one of the biggest department stores in town and who had wanted her, he had been really very sweet to her and bought her very expensive things, and he was a lot of fun for an old guy, but she didn't want any part of that, although he was the sweetest, kindest man and the best dancer in the world.

All small talk, McDonald had thought idly then, as he noted with hunger her healthy body, her hard legs, her crisp, clean movements, her bright, happy eyes as if she were on her first date.

They kissed that night and two nights later they went to bed.

"You want to make love to me, don't you?" she said, turning to look down at him as he nuzzled her flaccid drooping breasts.

He, startled, forced a smile and then a look of sensitive want from his sweaty concentration and said, "Yes."

"Why do you?" And she looked into his eyes, holding his head away—he finding out later that she believed a look directly in the eyes meant honesty.

"Because I like you very much, and you're a beautiful woman."

"You're a handsome man, too, Jim," she said, "and I'd like to go to bed with you but I really can't. You'll talk."

"No I won't . . . darling."

"I've got my reputation to keep in this town. You don't know how this town is. You've got to keep lily-white or every old biddy will keep after you till you can't take this town anymore. Nobody has ever said anything against me yet, and I won't give them the chance."

"I could never tell anyone."

"I know how men are after they've been to bed with a woman."

"Not me, Wanda. I promise."

"No. I can't. I just can't go to bed with you."

"Wanda, I need you. I want to make love to you."

"I know you do," she murmured, letting tenderness come into her eyes. "And I want to make love to you."

She went to see if her son was asleep and then they went to her bedroom where over her feebling hesitation he undressed her and then himself.

"You've got something to put on?"

"Yes."

She laughed. "I can tell you've been around," she said, glad.

She reclined upon the sheets, waiting.

"God, but you're wonderful. It's been so long, so terribly long," she cried, fastening upon him.

And afterwards, in a little-girl nasality, "What must you think of me? Knowing you only three days and then doing this?"

He held her tight and let the words out, darling, darling, you're wonderful, I think you're wonderful. Then they made love again.

They danced to the ancient tune; for three years they made love at their convenience.

After he studied and taught and graded papers and after her work, in the evenings they bucked to the old rhythm, in his apartment or hers, on beds or on couches, in his car, and he liked it, he remembered, he thought it was great, and she liked it too, she enjoyed his love-making, his love and enjoyment of her. The bed was their meeting ground, the sheets their conciliation and pleasure, the pillows their love.

He liked the idea that she was a kind of mistress, one he could not afford to keep, to be sure. He was proud, too, of the easiness and confidence he felt now that a woman was his.

They were sophisticated and casual about their other dating, as they liked to call it, he going with the bird-faced women instructors to affairs of the department and she going dancing with old men friends who called her up occasionally. He brushed shoulders and moments with bland-faced businessmen and gross-faced sergeants from the air base, and he believed he knew but did not question too much. Once, when he had protested her desire for a visitation to Omaha to see an old friend of hers, a man, he surmised, she had screamed at him, "Go to hell then, we're not married, you don't own me, you can't tell me what to do," and she had swept up her coat and flung out of his apartment, where she had ten minutes before lain on his bed. There had been a compensation: the next day the always inevitable hotly breathing splendid reconciliation.

They had talked with the word "love" upon their lips constantly, indeed it seemed every third word was "love": "I'd love to go with you," and "I love this steak," and "I love it like this," and "I love to do it with you," and "I love the way you look," and "I love you." In those last few months, after he got the job offer from Missouri, after she came to witness the Ph.D. getting and the handshake with the university chancellor, after the kiss upon his cheek she talked of love and marriage, how they could live on his salary and she could work too and save some money, and she never thought after all the trouble with her ex-husband (that bastard, as she usually called him) and the way he had treated her that she would ever be interested in marrying somebody else; "but I really love you, Jim," she said with a soulful look up into his eyes (that look denoting honesty).

He, well used to her by then, felt the loneliness of those first few months in Columbia, and they wrote often and feelingly, he pouring out his desire and that something akin to love to her; and thus he had rushed to her two years before.

The warehouses glided by, the sooty station emerged and slowed as the train clicked in with painful metal sounds.

There was a gleaming brightness to the sky and to the snow where the sun gave back diamond-hard glints of light.

McDonald descended with the herd of people and in an open space he set his suitcase down and opened it and took out one slender package wrapped in a Christmas paper with red bells and a red bow. He slipped the package into his topcoat pocket and checked in his bag at the lockers in the station. He looked around for a phone booth, his hand pleasantly playing with the package in his pocket, the package holding a pair of tan suede gloves, quite expensive, that he knew she would like, for she liked expensive things, gifts of any kind really, but especially expensive ones.

He called but there was no answer at her number, so he took a try at the office.

Her voice was unmistakable, and he felt again that queer little stir in his chest, a palpable motion of that which felt good, whether he might want it to feel good or not.

"Hi," he said. "This is Jim . . ." and in the fragment of the pause that followed, thinking that she would not know which Jim, ". . . McDonald. Hello, Wanda."

"Why, Jim!" she said, her voice coming to him pleased. "How are you?"

"Fine."

"It's been a long time since I've heard from you, stranger."

"About two years, Wanda."

"Has it really been that long?" (She was not much for remembering dates, he thought.)

"Yes, that long. I've thought about you a lot."

"And I've thought about you. You're here in town, aren't you?"

"Yes, at the train depot."

"Wonderful. You going to be here long?"

He hesitated, not quite expecting that question. "Just tonight, I guess. I'm on my way home."

"Sort of passing through then?"

"Yes," he said.

"Can you get away from work? I'd like to see you tonight."

"Oh," she said, "I really have a date tonight." She paused, and in the moment of her silence he heard muted telephonic clicks and buzzes and voices as from far distant places. "But I'll break the date," she said.

"Good," he said with greater relief than he could have thought possible.

"I'm really busy right now," she said. "So I'll come pick you up in about an hour. I have a car now you know."

"A car! Really? You must be prosperous these days," he said, and they laughed without knowing why. "Pick me up at Hermie's, can you?"

"Sure thing," she said sweetly.

He went out into the clean December air. The cold was sharp but he didn't mind, for the sun was bright and the sky a magnified blue. He walked up the street to the little tavern and had a beer and two cigarettes. Nobody knew him there, not even the corpulent gray bartender who had cashed his personal checks freely in the time before. He felt it again, the old unease of loneliness, and how bitingly it came upon him, speaking past chills and emptiness, and a woman could lift that all from him, a woman, a love, a connection. The little Falcon pulled up in the slush outside the blue bar windows, and McDonald went out without finishing his second beer. He felt good because she was his woman again, everybody could see that if they wanted to look, that she was there waiting for him. He thought he could see through the darkened window that she was still a good-looking woman, and the men in the bar would surely notice that, those lonely men would see that he was not lonely any longer.

The first moment was halting as he opened the door and stooped to get in. The large dark eyes, the white skin seeming whiter now, the high cheekbones, the careful deft coloring of lips and cheeks, the long slender neck, the deep brunette hair. And too he noted the hints of olding, the more pronounced hollow of the cheeks, the hardness of the jaws, the little compression around the mouth, and more than suggestion of wrinkles by the eyes, the dark hair too dark.

She was near to thirty-five, he thought, as he slid in, smiling brightly at her. She was still a good enough looking woman, but somehow not quite as he had imagined, and he thought perhaps he had been imagining too long, all the way from Columbia, how it would be.

"You look very good, Wanda," he said.

"Thank you, Jim," she said, smiling. "I need somebody to say that to me after a day at work."

"You're as good-looking as you were five years ago when we first met," he went on, hearing himself turn casually to glibness and lies and excusing himself instantly by acknowledging that he too was five years older and what difference did a little flattery make?

She touched his hand with hers. "You look pretty good yourself. College teaching must agree with you."

He laughed, a sudden, skittish sound. "Yes. I gained ten pounds."

"It looks fine on you."

She drove slowly and carefully, for the streets were filled with slush beginning to freeze again. He asked about her job and she told him her complaints, how she should be getting paid more, and about all the things she had to do, and how she had heard some elevator operators say she was the best secretary in the whole building and her boss knew it too; her voice became petulant and peevish, and he remembered hearing that voice and that similar complaint many times, and he wished she would talk of something else.

"If you stop at the market I'll get us a steak," he broke in.

"Would you," she said. "I have to get some things there anyway." They stopped and he ran in, after she had laughingly said to get enough meat because Trevor was getting big as a horse and ate like one. He got a pint of whiskey, just in case, with a what-the-hell feeling like from the other time, and they went on to her place, a duplex at the east end of the city, the same place where she had moved the spring of the year he left for Columbia.

The boy, Trevor, opened the door for them. He was taller, thinner, his eyes and eyelids still dark and somber. He was coming to pimples and self-consciousness. "Well," he said, surprised, "Jim McDonald. Hi, Jim." All with good will, and McDonald was relieved at that, although there had never been any hostility between them.

In the living room the Christmas tree glowed with tender blue and red; McDonald gave a murmuring comment on it as he carried the grocery packages through to the kitchen.

"Trevor and I put it up and trimmed it," Wanda said. "Isn't it a beauty? I just love a nice big Christmas tree."

While Wanda prepared the meal McDonald went upstairs with the son and looked at the model cars and airplanes that the boy had built, the hobby that McDonald had started him on three years before. The boy stood there, waiting half-embarrassedly, wanting to be praised and McDonald gave him praise enough. (That was cheap enough and easy to give, he thought, especially to the boy, who he had never realized until that moment was quite so young. Lonesome, self-conscious boy with the self-protective curve of shoulders beginning, the wounds of eyes. Named Trevor whimsically, "because it sounded good," Wanda had said. "I love pretty things and pretty sounds.") They went down and ate when Wanda called. The boy talked about school and the things he was building in shop class and the dance steps he was learning. After dinner the boy sat in discomfort and looked at them.

"Why don't you go to a movie?" Wanda said to him.

"I don't want to go alone," the boy said.

"Well, take somebody, one of your buddies, for god sakes, if you don't want to go alone." She looked at McDonald who at the hint dug through his wallet and gave the boy enough money for two passes and bus fare.

"Come straight home," Wanda said, and when he had left she turned to McDonald and said, "Isn't he a wonderful boy? I just love him so much. He's going to be so tall and handsome."

"A real girl-killer," McDonald said idly.

"And how," she said. "Trevor's about everything I live for. I want so much for him. I love him. It's hard for a man to understand how much a woman can love her child." She looked away, pensively. "I suppose you have to carry a baby beneath your heart to know," with a little catch of breath.

McDonald coughed and lit a cigarette, watching the match glow, anxious not to observe this deceit. She had moments of frenzied motherhood, he knew, times of raging motherly passion, soon over, soon spent, but in those moments she screamed of her love and struck out at him if he even slightly demurred.

"I want to see your Christmas tree again," he said, anxious to leave the closeness of that room, and they went out into the living room. The tree glowed softly, pleasantly, and there were several packages beneath the branches.

"Trevor did most of it," she said. "I never knew he could enjoy anything so much. But we both like this season so much. It's such a beautiful season. Isn't it wonderful, when everybody's so happy and things are so nice and pretty?"

"When everybody loves everybody else," he said.

"That's it, isn't it?" she said. "Everybody so loving and happy. Trevor and I are going to go to church on Christmas Eve. It was his idea, can you imagine that?" She laughed. "I told him he was going to turn out to be a preacher if he didn't look out."

McDonald smiled and surveyed the room, noting the new stereo set, the new TV, the chinaware, the picture of Wanda's mother and father prominently on the television, the picture taken on their fortieth wedding anniversary, the group of pictures of Trevor at varying ages on the little cupboard.

"Oh, you haven't seen the new furniture, have you?" she said, following his glance. She went to the new stereo set and put on some records. "This and the television are compliments of Trevor's father. He got killed in a car accident in Wisconsin, and the insurance went to Trevor, and Trevor gets the old man's Social Security, too. So Jack (the father's name, McDonald remembered) after all these years of not giving a damn about Trevor finally came through after all."

Christmas carols floated out around them from the record player.

"Well," McDonald began, and then added lamely, "that's good."

"That's what I say. You might as well get as much as you can, and he did pretty well for Trevor, now it turns out. Trev didn't know what to do with all that insurance money, so I said why don't you get something nice for the house for when you have your friends over. What he wanted most were the hi-fi and the TV. They're his."

"Nice sets," McDonald murmured.

"They're the best," she said. "I saw to that. I think the best isn't good enough. For now on I'm only going for what's best for me." She smiled suddenly. "What would you say if I got married one of these days?"

He jerked as if something hot had touched him. "That's sudden," he said. "I thought you weren't interested in marrying again."

"I'm getting tired of working for a living," she said. "I think I may latch onto some rich old fuddy-duddy one of these days and devote myself to cooking and housecleaning, permanently."

"And to the bedroom?" he said.

She laughed, loud and energetically, as she always laughed at anything remotely off-color that pleased her. "That most of all," she said.

"We'll drink to that," he said. He got the bottle from his coat and went to the kitchen to make drinks. Wanda was lounging on the couch when he returned. She had earlier changed into slacks and a sweater. She was listening to the stereo carol "Silent Night" with composure, and her mouth changed into a smile when she saw him and they touched glasses and drank.

"You always could make the best drinks," she said.

"Thanks," he said. He sat on the edge of the sofa, his hip touching her calves. The slacks she wore were tight and he looked frankly at her smooth legs.

"Speaking of marriage, how come you're not?" she said.

"Oh, I don't know," he said, thinking distantly of the women he had gone with since he had last seen Wanda; there had been two seductions and brief dalliances, the seductions possible, he now reflected, because it grew easier as one grew older. There had been nothing of vitality with either of those two distant women, only a studied casualness in the use of each other's bodies; he had tried to put more there, make something good come of it, but they had withdrawn, broken it off as if he had committed a violation or broken a casual rule. He did not talk of them.

"I'd think some little coed would snap you up in no time."

He laughed. "You flatter me."

"I would if I were one of your students," she said. "And I bet I'd get A's from you too."

"Probably you would," he said agreeably.

"People have gone to bed for a hell of a lot less than an A on a report card," she said, giving her loud, flat laugh. "I wish I'd gone on to college, instead of going to that damn business school—or instead of getting married at eighteen like I did. I would have been a good student, too. I always wanted to learn."

He sipped on his drink.

"Wouldn't I have been good?" she prodded.

"Yes," he said, looking into the pale amber of ice cubes and whiskey in his glass.

"I know I would have been," she said. "God knows where I'd be if I'd had a little education, you know, like people get nowadays." She drank a little. "How do you like teaching now?" she asked.

She had never quite understood what colleges or college teaching were about, he thought, saw it somewhat like an extension of her recollection of high school, and so he abbreviated his duties for her.

"What I especially wanted was to get in some faculty wives club," she said. "I'd like to punch their noses, the bitches. They're all so snobbish and they think they're so good."

"I didn't know you knew any," he said.

"Oh, I see them all right. They come hotsy-totsying down to the office, teetering on their high heels, looking down their noses at everybody. They don't see me, though. They just pretend they can see right through a secretary. If they only knew what I know about them!"

He fondled the glass and thought, it was a victory for her, too, to seduce me, to have her period of going with someone supposedly intellectual, to go with "a professor from the university," as she had always liked to refer to him to her easily astonished friends.

"They spell out their names for you as though you're illiterate. They act as if you can't read, for god's sake."

"Have you read any books lately?" he asked, wanting to change the subject.

"I haven't had time. Good heavens, I've been so busy at the office and getting Trevor off to school and keeping him going and making all the payments it's almost more than one person can do. I've thought about getting another job to go along with the one I've got, but I don't think I could do it all. This summer Trevor's going to work a little and earn some of his own money. You don't know how lucky you've got it, being a free and easy bachelor without a care in the world. You should try raising a son sometime, seeing that he's properly dressed and has money and a good home. A young person needs an education and nice things and a nice place to bring his friends, and I'm doing that for Trev."

The phone rang and Wanda got up, patting his shoulder and smiling at him. She talked very softly and briefly and she said she had company and couldn't go out, and no she couldn't go out later in the evening either and was very sorry but would you call back later in the week? McDonald felt the quick charge of jealousy, seeing in his long absence the succession of men, seeing now that young man hunched over a phone perhaps in a booth in a downtown barroom, the young man speaking persuasively, laconically, McDonald seeing himself too and the same conversation he had had on occasion with Wanda, his impatience, his want, and how he too had been put off at the times of her assignations—everything always vigorously denied by her, and couldn't he trust her more? she asked in that wistful, little-girl voice she assumed at times like that—but assignations nonetheless. He felt the spirited surge of anger jump through his belly, and he calmed himself immediately, telling himself it was foolish to feel that now of all times, knowing what his own purpose was. No, no, he said to himself, there was more than that here, an affection, something good and lasting, perhaps even a love of a sort, there really was . . . He very casually lit a cigarette and drew on it, and calmly cupped the drink in the other hand.

All the careful disconcern to show he had not listened, and that it had not affected him, made no difference for she blandly told him when she returned.

"That was Frank Wykoff," she said, taking up her drink as she reclined upon the couch. "He brought me that Royal Doulton, those three mugs up there (pointing to the mantle), from England when he was there a couple of months ago." The mugs grinned fat and hideous from among the plastic planters.

"He brings me nice, expensive things. I don't know why he does it."

"He's in the service then?" McDonald asked.

"He's a sergeant in the ground crew and he goes overseas whenever the wing is rotated. He's going to bring me some linens and stuff from Ireland next time he gets to England, he said. He brings me something nice every time he comes back."

"Well, that's nice," McDonald said.

"I think so. You know how much I like nice, pretty things, and expensive things especially. Frank has brought me lace from Spain and perfume from France and that Royal Doulton."

"He can get it all from any px in England," McDonald said, and was surprised at the grumbling petulance in his voice.

"Well it's the real article to me," she said. "I don't know why he does it. I guess he likes me and he's lonesome and wants somebody to talk to."

"That's probably it," McDonald said.

"When he's here at the base he calls me up all the time, wanting to take me out dancing or to dinner. He wants to spend all his money on me. I'm not going to stop him." She was looking at McDonald, and she was trying to gauge him, he knew. "I think you'd like him a lot. He's only twenty-four, a mere child. I keep telling him he should pick up some girl his own age and have a great time, but he doesn't want to. He couldn't believe I had a son fourteen; he thought I was his age." She laughed loudly, and McDonald smiled too. "Frank told me I was the only woman he's met that was like European women. And he just likes me. There's nothing more between us, he just likes me. He's a nice boy who buys me nice things and takes me out to nice places and we have a good time. He doesn't really mean a thing to me, but he's lonesome, and anyway he's too young for anything serious!" The pleased, shrill, too-loud laugh again.

There was a pause and they heard the music suddenly, the carols past, Dinah Washington singing now, and Wanda swayed her head in time to the sentimental Negro song.

"Dance?" he said, and she smiled and nodded and swiveled out of the couch and stood up and they took a step or two; her hair touched his chin and her sweater his chest. He stopped the movement and kissed her and her mouth opened a little.

"I'd like to make love to you," he said.

"Ah ah," she said, shaking her head and her forefinger at him. "I know about guys like you. Got an old girlfriend in a town and they visit her once a year or so, and expect her to fall over."

He smiled at her, affectedly, out of the same concentration he had felt that first time, so long ago now, and he knew why it had come about, how it had led to this, the same want and need, the same panic at denial.

"I thought it was a good idea," he said.

"Anyway, I can't, because Trevor might come home."

"He went to a movie, remember?"

"Oh Jim," she said, "I don't want something to start up between us again that might turn out badly."

"I didn't think it turned out badly before," he murmured slowly. What else could he say? he asked himself. Somewhere deep within he heard a distant door slam, an echo of another time. The want of her unbalanced all.

"Well no, it was fine, but you got so jealous there a few times, and you're so intense."

"I promise not to be so intense," he said, giving her a smile.

"Do you really want to make love to me?" she asked, putting on her incongruous little-girl face, and little-girl voice, trying to look pensively up through her eyelashes.

"Yes. Don't you want to?"

"Yes. Only with you."

He kissed her.

"Fix one more drink, then," she said, and they went to the kitchen together. "Nobody can fix drinks like you can," she said.

He wanted to say, you've said that, but instead they touched glasses and drank to each other.

"You want to see the upstairs as I've got it done new?" she asked.

He nodded and followed her up the steps. They looked perfunctorily at the boy's room and the bath and then they went to the next room. "This is still my bedroom," she said.

The room was spotless, for she believed that cleanliness was a great virtue, he remembered. There was a group photograph of her family on her dresser and a series of pictures of Trevor upon the wall.

"It looks very nice," he said. "You've rearranged it."

"I've pushed the furniture around several times since you were last here," she said.

"That was a long time ago. You haven't seen the room for a long time, have you?"

"No, I haven't."

"A little anxious, aren't you?" she asked archly, teasing him.

"Yes."

"What time is it?"

He looked at his watch. "A little after eight."

"We have time then."

She unbuckled her belt and slid down her tight slacks. There were the silk panties, the long smooth legs, marred by the slight faintly darkened beginning clusters of varicose veins which he saw and then purposely did not look at. The sweater came next, the arms lifted, the sigh of clothing, the sigh of the woman, and the careful folding of the sweater and slacks over the chair. Poised forward, her arms behind her, the hands reached for the brassiere connection.

"I'll do it," he said.

"Your hands are cold," she said, startled, and let him undo her.

She turned; the sagging breasts, flattened, a flanged brownness around the nipple, and the soft sag beneath. The soft protrusion of belly as the nylon panties were slid down, and she went beneath the blanket.

"It's a little chilly," she said. "I'm cold. Hurry up."

He took off his clothes and went in beside her, as she lifted the sheet and closed it again over them.

The telephone began to ring downstairs. "Damn," she said. "I should have taken it off the hook."

"You want to go answer it?"

"No. It's probably for Trevor anyway. He's in the telephone-hanging stage now, wants to talk for hours with his friends. They call him up at all hours, I can hardly get to use the phone any-more. He's starting to go out with girls now, too, and they're aggressive little devils these days; they call him all the time." The telephone rang eight times (a part of his brain counted that), and she talked on about Trevor and what he was doing and how he was coming along in school and how much she loved him and she was going to make a man out of him.

While McDonald felt along the smoothness of her thighs to the crisp hair and she moved her legs to let him finger her.

"Trevor's getting along fine with the girls," she was saying. "They're just crazy about him." She moved a little. "Have you got something on?"

"Yes," he said, thinking that there was not even a cursory inspection, that she would demand care and cleanliness if he were to probe her ear orifice with his finger, but no demand at all to probe this part of her.

She slid toward him as he moved over her.

"It's been a long time for us, hasn't it?"

"Two years," he said.

There was a little pressure at first and then it was all right.

"You're very nice and warm," she said. "God, has it been cold here. Is it this cold in Columbia?"

"Not quite," he murmured.

"Um, you feel good," she said. She looked at his body, him lifted over her.

"This was always nice. Like old times."

"Yes."

She put her arms under his and her hands felt his hips. She moved her hips gradually, quickening a little, and shortly and easily, as she always could, he remembered, she went, clenching her teeth and eyes, giving a sort of subdued groan, and then she relaxed, opened her eyes and smiled at him.

"You could always make me do it easily," she said, and gave a sigh, as if they had recently finished a passably good dish of ice cream, he thought. "Now you do it," she said.

Beneath him the flaccid body waited, the shoulders moved a little each time upon the sheets, the calm, impassive, pretty face looked placidly past his shoulder. Gradual quickening. Two minutes, three, and she lifted her legs to accept him, gauging him expertly he thought; and then drawing himself together to push, not energetically, it was over.

They were not even perspiring, he thought.

"That was nice," she said.

They dressed and went downstairs to finish their drinks.

"How is your writing going?" she asked in the composure of the living room, the Christmas carols afresh on the record player.

"I'm not doing much," he said. Like many men who had gone into literature he had thought at one time that he could write and he had even gotten a couple of stories into little magazines. She had been terrifically impressed by the printed page with his name on it, had even bought copies of the magazine for herself, although as far as he knew she had read only one story he had ever written and that one had depressed her.

("You're so *intense* about everything, Jim," she had said. She had liked that adjective, intense, had used it often thereafter. "Why do you write about such dark and unhappy things? You should take things more lightly.")

"You should keep writing, Jim," she said now. "You're really talented."

"I wish I were," he said.

"You are talented," she cried. "You should write." She had always liked that idea, he thought, along with the intellectual side of him, the thought that perhaps he would someday write a successful novel. "You must keep writing." She laughed and in enthusiasm struck his shoulder. "You should write about me. God, that would be a best seller."

Her story, she called it. She felt that "her story" was something unique, somehow enormously interesting if it could be written down; just to do "her story," farm girl come to the city of Lincoln, Nebraska, to take a course in a business college, after the wedding in wartime and the divorce, to become a secretary and live in a duplex, shoddily rear a son, and be seduced by men. Although Wanda could never bring herself to say it, McDonald knew that the excitement of "her story" revolved around the men she had known and slept with; it was a secret pride with her.

In those first days of their love-making, in their sophisticated detachment and disinterest, they had talked about men and woman, and with bland inquisitiveness, not really caring, not as he cared in the sharper inquisitions later on, he had asked her about the men, and always she had lied, or so he presumed from the variations in her stories. First there had been but three, the husband who had robbed her of virginity, a school principal from Albion who had helped her recover from loneliness and divorce, and after several years of a growing virtue came McDonald; another time there had been eight, again there had been eleven, and once in acute honesty, for she could never remember her lies about that, she had said "about fifteen" but she could not remember the names of one or two. "It was kind of like brushing teeth, the importance of it," he said to her in half-jest, and she was irritated by that, and the next time he called for her she had put him off, saying, "If I'm no more important than brushing teeth to you, I guess you don't want to go with me," but later she came around to his cajolery, and whimpered a little and said she had made it all up about the men she had known, it was all a lie, a little white one, and she was hurt that he hadn't realized that, for didn't everybody like to exaggerate a little? So she reverted to the story of but three men in her life, with a fourth and most important—Trevor, of course. It was then McDonald began to feel a nagging hurt in his belly, a distemper hot and unpredictable, as if some ancient and honest pain had risen and fastened itself upon him.

McDonald shook his head at that hurt that he felt again, and she, misinterpreting it, said, "Don't give up on your writing now. Keep at it."

The virtue of hard work, he thought. Perseverance will bring you through to success and especially fortune (which can buy such nice, expensive things) is what she always believed.

Suddenly somber, he drank his drink and went to fix another. He wished to get drunk and knew he could not, not that night.

"Where's the good feeling we're supposed to have?" he asked suddenly and sharply.

"What do you mean?" she asked, looking queerly at him.

"Where's that gaiety, that spirit, that life tonight? We've had our drinks, danced our dance, made our love." The knot of that old distemper grew hotter and harder.

"Have things been so bad tonight?" she asked with female defensiveness. "I'm sorry if after two years there isn't the red carpet. You've gotten a lot for nothing. What do you expect?"

He shook his head. "Nothing," he said.

They were in it together, he thought, together they had reached this conclusion, together had formulated this hypocrisy in the desert of their dead hearts, in this grotesquery of passion and of feeling; the heart bursting with love and clutching for love, the body writhing in the soft agony of lustful energy, wanting love, all succumbed to the heartbreaking most common ordeal of her bed. Passionless, passionless, he cried to himself. The dull embrace, the plodding ritual, absent the feeling, absent the bond. They had made themselves what they were. With haughty dreams of sophistication they had found each other, with sham they seduced each other, used each other, in this parody of love their hearts had become gargoyles, blandly reducing all to this commonplace ordeal.

He had known it all, that there was no more than this, he had known it but he had not believed it. He had needed to come here this time to find out. And the wry revelation struck him like a blow on his forehead. The energy of their listless bodies, their dull lust, their passionless pretensions could not make them whole.

He felt unclean, like a fat, briefcase-carrying businessman dropping through town to surreptitiously and dispassionately satisfy neither love nor lust, but to bulwark his pretense.

"So what have we got now?" he cried again and closed his eyes.

"We've got a great deal," she said.

"We have? You and I?" his voice croaked.

"I don't understand you at all," she said, the hostility rising in her eyes and face. "Even if we possessed each other—if we were married, what would we have?" Who has said that this sexual combat could save us all? he asked himself, who has said the thrust of loins, the twin orgasms, the clenched teeth, the straining muscles, the bleats and sweat at night would redeem us? What blasphemy was this, dissolved into the routine placation, the casual embrace, the promiscuous ritual, the ugly usage?

"I would not use an animal or a machine as we have used each other," he said.

"Used!" she said, in astonishment at him, her eyes coating with tears. "I have not used you. I haven't." She turned her face against the wall and began to cry. "I'm sorry I displeased you so much," she sobbed. "Now that you have what you want you dislike me."

"Wanda, Wanda," he said, shaking his head, as he looked at her distorted white face, wrenching its tears into her thin hands. They had made themselves ciphers, he thought, routine memories to be counted up. To her new men friends she would say he was the college professor who had "loved" her and had courted her and would have married her too but she didn't want to, she wanted to keep her independence, a man who was nice enough and treated her well and bought her nice things, but didn't mean a thing to her; and in the company of friends he would be, if she came to talk of it, that intellectual companion that she had known who was going to write her story; and in the remote, occasional honest depths he was the man—only man, not love, not lover—

who had exchanged orgasms with her for three years and twice thereafter. To him she was the woman who had been his mistress during his time in graduate school (his "shack-up" to those more gross), whom he could visit when back in town (in his under-graduate days he had seen two dormitory janitors talking, two ancient, gnarled, ugly old men with gold-rimmed glasses and dentures, who had looked at the girlie picture on a student's wall, and the one said, "I can remember when I held a woman like that in my arms," and McDonald could see himself with that prostatic, arthritic clutch, spittle erupting along his thin and ancient brown lips, saying to himself, "Yes, I held such a one naked in my arms one day," the beautiful young woman, Wanda).

"Ciphers," he said. Indistinguishable ciphers in the routine of friendship, reduced by their sophistication to this. "No passion or energy or excitement or love," he said slowly and viciously, while she simply stared at him, her eyes red from crying. "What have we made? What have we got? Five years of this and what? . . ."

The boy banging open the door, letting the rush of cold air in, moved them to stand and go to the other room. The boy was red-cheeked and sniffly from the cold. Stiffly, almost with careful politeness, they talked about the movie he'd seen and a little later the boy said goodnight and went upstairs to bed.

Wanda smiled at McDonald; the tears had not been vigorous or deep.

"I'm sorry you feel that way," she said. "You always were so intense."

"Yes," he said.

Her hand touched his with surprising hotness. "You can stay here if you want to," she said. "Trevor will sleep late and I can fix you breakfast and take you to the station in the morning."

"What will the neighbors say?"

"They better not say anything, the nosey bitches. I don't care what they think anyway." She smiled suddenly. "Anyway, they've seen you here before."

"What about Trevor?" he asked, remembering the times they had made love with the boy sleeping in the next room, or how they had frozen when he had gone to the bathroom, and there they waited in strange posture until he returned to his bedroom.

"Trevor knows what it's all about," she said.

"He knows about you and me?"

"Well, we've never talked about it, if that's what you mean," she said with a laugh, "but he should know. If he doesn't know what grown people do with sex, then it's high time he found out."

It takes a wise son to know his mother, McDonald thought, smiling too. And what are you, James R. McDonald? he asked.

"No," he said abruptly. "I've got to go. I can catch a late train."

"Don't you want to stay for a little while?"

"No, Wanda," he said, going to her, kissing her compressed mouth one time. He got his coat and put it on.

"I will see you again?" she asked, with her wistful face on again.

"I don't know," he said, and went to the door.

"I don't want to see you go like this," she said. "I think you might be angry."

"I'm not angry."

"Write me," she said. "Write me, won't you? I really miss those letters you used to send." Her eyes were suddenly stricken, as if she too saw the loss of it all, the recognition of what they did not have and had never had.

"I'll see you again, won't I?" she asked, and then she looked acutely at him, with a sardonic perceptiveness that frightened him, and said, "Yes, I'll see you again." She patted his shoulder almost maternally and she said, "Write me," and called almost as an afterthought, "Merry Christmas," through the closing door.

He went out into the bitter cold, into the gray dirty night with the snow gray and ugly upon the cruel landscape. He huddled into his coat, feeling in his pocket the soft and crackly package with the gloves for Wanda, and he thought of returning and giving them to her, but he changed his mind, shook his head, said to himself, no, let it be as it is. He walked on, down the street where the houses huddled like cringing dogs against the cold, and he bent his head into the wind, walking toward the sore of light reflected above the center of the city.

The Metal Sky

It was early when he brought the tractor down the hill from the farmstead to cultivate the corn. The cultivator hung on the tractor like a spider, moving and jerking and groaning with the movements of the tractor. It was cool in the hollow by the ditch, and the heavy dew hung in silent and plastic rainbow-colored droplets from the willows and from the bayonetshaped corn leaves, and when the tractor raced through, the droplets shattered and rained on the tractor and on the blue denim legs of the man who was driving. The tractor went fast and the black earth curled up and turned like something alive before the cultivator shovels.

The ditch was broad and steep. It had been part of a pasture, but the man had plowed the fertile hill and put it in crops and then he had cut a few of the willows that grew in thicket-like profusion along the bank and had planted corn there too. There were still willows growing in the ditch and struggling along the edges of the bank. There was no water there except with heavy rains, and sometimes a puddle stood for days, hidden in weeds at the bottom of the ditch and hovered over by yellow butterflies.

The noise of the tractor was very loud in the hollow and the birds in the willows scattered when the tractor came by. The man turned at the end of the field and swung back into the corn and the shovels spun the earth up, loosening the earth and shaking it, and he worked near the edge of the bank, the large hind wheel of the tractor skirting the weed cover there.

The bank gave way almost soundlessly and leisurely far behind the tractor, and the earth slid quietly down into the ditch, and the moving crust of bank ate away and pursued the tractor. The man was looking forward and he did not see it eating away behind him, and he felt it finally, the escaping earth tugging at the wheel. He looked and saw the almost casual destruction below him and he swung the wheel of the tractor hard, away from the bank, but this gesture only assisted the moving earth, for it threw the weight on the outer wheel. The front of the tractor rose and the spider arms of the cultivator sprang into the air above the corn, and the bright steel shovels glittered, and then with the sigh of the escaping earth the tractor slid and rolled and fell. The man held the wheel and he tried to move with the roll of the tractor but the steel bars caught him and pulled him in and he was held there, vised in between the wheel and the earth in the ditch.

The sun was looking at him when he recovered consciousness. It was all he could see at first, the hard and insistent yellow eye probing him. And around the sun the sky was a polished and bright metal blue. It occurred to him that he was yet in bed and the sun was already up and he strove suddenly to move, and it was then he felt that other insistent scalpel touch in his legs, and he remembered. He lay on his side, and his right arm was twisted under him and his face was burrowed partially into the hard dry earth; his face had struck the pebbly wash of the ditch. His legs were beneath the wheel of the silent tractor; he felt a great numbness there, broken by flashing and gritty sharpness at intervals. He tried to fix the moments of sharpness and he discovered that they came whenever he breathed. When he held his breath the pain did not come at all, there was only the rather satisfying numbness.

He was aware of a gurgling sound nearby and he lifted his head with great effort and looked about him. The sound was from the gasoline tank slowly leaking the fuel. The gasoline dribbled out around the closed cap and streaked down the painted metal and made a little pool in the ditch, at the man's elbow. The tank had been full, he thought, it would take a little while to empty, and he tried to think how long he had been there by the way the tank was emptying. There would be help soon, he thought, as soon as he was missed there would be help. He felt his overall bib for the pocket watch and he labored with the fob, dragging the watch out, but it was smashed. The hands had even been driven off, and the hands pointed nowhere from the bottom of the crushed crystal. The man looked dumbly at the watch, and he felt the smashed, still creased-together crystal, as if it were impossible that the watch could not run. The man squinted at the sun, and it too looked like a watch dial. The sun hung over his head, but it could not be noon, he thought, and he looked again and the sun was directly over him. If it is noon, they will surely miss him, he thought, and they will come searching for him, and this knowledge made him feel a little better. It was hot and the sweat streaked into his eyes and smarted, blinding him at moments and then all he could see was the blurred yellowness of the sun. There was great heat and the sun seemed to focus on him, the heat and the light white and hot and blinding, and he knew it was just his imagination, the sun was the sun and it was always hot and it did not choose to focus on anyone or anything. He would have loved that heat before, he thought, the sunlight that pulled the growing corn and fattened the growing animals, and warmly rubbed his shoulders when he was on the tractor. The sun did not choose him to burn, he thought, and yet it was too hot.

The sharpness in his legs was coming more quickly now, and it was rising, too, feeling up to his thighs, and he tried to recall the connection he had worked out before and he remembered his breathing. He was breathing very quickly and each time there was the sharp hurt, climbing from his legs to his hips, and he tried to slow his breathing, but he could not. The sun, it is too hot, he thought, and he remembered his hat, but the hat had fallen some-where. He lifted his head and looked carefully and slowly about him. To lift his head caused him great pain. The straw hat rested against the foxtail beyond the wash, perhaps two yards from him. One end of it was tipped up and the hat swayed from time to time as little breezes eddied down the gulley. The man looked at the hat and he watched, straining his head and eyes to see it. The man did not feel any of the breezes that moved the hat, and it was as if the foxtail swayed of their own accord and thus swayed the hat with them. The man reached for the hat but it was far far beyond him.

The exertion wore upon him and he turned his head down again. The sun poured down. He felt the heat and he closed his eyes to rest. But there was another yellowness and he squinted and saw the sun very close to him and very bright and hot. It glit-tered and it moved and swayed delicately. The sun had moved, he thought, and he looked where the sun was supposed to be and it was still there. The other light was the sun reflected clearly from the shiny metal that the pouring gasoline had cleansed and he could not look anywhere now without the sun being there.

Perhaps he could dig, he thought, perhaps there was loose dirt beneath his legs and he could pull himself away to the shade. He reached along his body and touched the area where the pain was growing to and he felt the earth beneath his legs. It was hard and dry and pebbly there in the wash of the gulley. He dug there and even his hard, calloused hands could do nothing; he scratched at the ground and made a little hole that he could just put his hand into, after great exertion, but his hand was bleeding then and exhaustion came on him. He cursed to himself, he cursed the hard dry ground and he cursed the tractor with its weight upon him and he cursed the pain and the land and the hard yellow sun. He let his head drop upon the pebbly earth and the sun lavished its yellow heat upon him.

The low strange sound awoke him; it was a heavy sound, like a groan or a sigh and he heard it dimly and listened and it was close to him. He thought of men coming in search for him, with shovels and strength to free him, but the sound was too strange and too heavy and he knew then it was himself, breathing, and he could listen to himself as from a distance. He moved his body slightly and the instant pain shot through him and seemed to burst in fire through his skull. He was truly awake then, and the heat was very heavy upon his face. He knew he was badly burned and he tried to pull his shirt up to cover his face, but he could not pull it far enough and if he moved too much the pain from his legs came driving up so that he could not do anything. Breathing was beginning to be hard for him now. The sun had moved slightly, he thought, for the reflection from the tractor was dull, and yet the sun was there, still above him. He looked across the sky for clouds, for the floating cotton clumps that collected on summer afternoons and sometimes glowered together to cause rain. But there were no clouds. The sky was hot and blue, shaped like a metal plate and with the color of the flame of a gasoline burner, and the blue became pale and brittled and yellow around the watch-dial sun.

He thought there were sounds and he listened. It was mid-afternoon and they would surely be looking for him, he thought. He pictured them coming through the corn rows and following the tractor tracks and noticing the cave-off beside the ditch. And he remembered he had told no one that he would be cultivating the corn in the hollow; the day before he had worked in the upper fields, and if he were missed, the children and the wife would go there first. And here, he thought, the ground dried quickly and the tractor tracks were obliterated by the harrow teeth that followed the wheels of the tractor, and there were the protective, hiding clumps of willows. Because of the trees it was difficult to see far along that winding ditch. There the clusters of willows and the tall weeds and cave-offs were frequent; the rains often undermined the banks and pulled the earth in and perhaps they would not detect this place where the fallen earth was already dried and where it looked like an ancient wound in the bank. The man turned his head to scan the bank and there were trees up there, protecting the slide, and only a very observant one would even notice. But they will have to come soon now, he thought.

He listened above the growing concentration of distractions that he knew was pain that grew in his brain. The birds were chattering and flitting among the willows and they were singing. The birds had been silent for a long time after the accident, or perhaps he did not hear before, the man thought. The birds were there in groups and they were singing, as they sang on any afternoon. And the breeze moved through the willows delicately, sinuously, moving the light-green leaves into tentacles, but the breeze did not reach the gulley bed, did not even touch the cattails and the Indian tobacco and the foxtail where the hat still rested.

The mid-afternoon sun tortured the earth around him and wilted the weeds and grass. And yet they did not come. He would shout, he thought, perhaps they would hear. He opened his mouth, but the tongue, foreign and huge, filled up the cavern, and he tried to shout, but his voice escaped drily and he could only croak something he could not understand. He tried to swallow, but the alkali dryness in his mouth prevented it. He croaked the sound again and was satisfied when the chattering birds hesitated in their noise. Perhaps they will yet hear, he thought, and he tried again with all his energy, and a few of the birds flew away this time. He tried again and again to make a sound, but he knew they were not shouts anymore. The birds came back and he could not even hear his voice above the raucous and cheerful noise they made.

His thirst was violent. The man moved himself on his elbow and he looked at the bed of the ditch. Near him the pool of gasoline glittered rainbow-colored in the sun, and as the gasoline evaporated it caused the light to shimmer and the colors to diffuse. A distance away there was a puddle of water, perhaps the size of a man's head, and a cluster of yellow butterflies moved above the muddy, tiny pool. The butterflies surged in and out, restlessly, and without any sound. They fluttered and turned and milled in the brilliant light of their own coloring so that it was impossible to distinguish them one from another. The butterflies arose suddenly and hovered in a mass above the bank, and the man raised his head to look at the water, only three arm's lengths away. Now that he saw the water clearly, the thirst grew worse, and even the evil pain in his legs was insignificant.

The butterflies returned. One felt the man's motion and came to flutter in his face. He felt the faint elastic brush upon his burning skin. He knew the butterflies did this to drive other moving creatures away; it was the season of their breeding. The legs walked coolly on his cheek and rested, and the gorgeous yellow wings moved ever so slightly to give it balance.

The man felt the butterfly there, and it was unconcerned, as if he were already dead. The man lifted his free hand slowly and he brought his fingers up and then very carefully and quickly snapped the fingers shut on the arched yellow wings. The butterfly struggled, but its wings were caught and its fragile black body vibrated in its writhings. The yellow dust on the wings rubbed off and filtered down, lightly.

It will know I am not dead, the man thought. It alone, if nothing else, will know. He held the fragile wings of yellow light, with the wings so delicate he could not even feel them between his hardened hands. The butterfly tried to move and could not and the claws of its legs clasped the air. Perhaps it thinks it is near death, the man thought, it has not been in this position before and it knows it is strange and terrible to be near death with nothing else around. How easy it is to give death, the man thought, how easy to crush out something, to say, "I give thee death." But how impossible it is to say, "I give thee life." What was once something, something perhaps delicate and beautiful, becomes nothing in that terrible and decisive moment of death, and there was nothing dead that was ever beautiful. And there is nothing anyone can ever do to change it. How little it took sometimes, and he thought of the usual afternoons in the field, and where he would be, cultivating the tall corn on the hills now, where there was a breeze and coolness, where the sun was warmly light on his shoulders, and where the crops grew, and the wind was caressing, and he remembered the water jugs and how he turned his face up and the cool water splashed over his face and down his shirt, and he remembered his son riding on the tractor with him, and it had been pleasant, for he took pride in that powerful machine, and in the good, rich soil, and in his son. But something had said, or they had conspired and said, "I give thee death," and in one moment of a usual morning, he lay half-crushed and enfeebled in the ditch.

He moved his fingers and he crushed the brittle butterfly. In one instant, now, the man thought, I give thee death, and the moment was gone, the instant, the now, already past, was irretrievable. He let the fragility fall, and there was still the light-yellow smudge of the wing coloring covering the blood on the man's fingertips.

The sun was like a white-hot hammer on his skull. The pain of his legs had settled to a heavy and throbbing sharpness. His mouth was arid and his lips were beginning to crack. He was aware of a labored, groaning sound when he worked to take a breath. And the worst was the sun and the metal sky.

It was as if he could feel his brain shrinking and drying out and beginning to flake off in little feathers of nothingness. It was then he thought that he would die. He knew no one would come. If it would only rain, he thought, if there would only be water.

He began to go under for moments and he did not want to lose consciousness, and he fought it, but gradually it overcame him and he would start into consciousness again and nothing would be changed. The sun hung in the same place, and the birds chattered and the breezes moved the top branches of the willows.

Two sparrows dropped from the trees and hung upon the hemp weeds, and their bright black eyes noted the man and forgot him, and the birds hit the pebbly wash of the ditch in a tangle of grayness and feathers, breeding. The female fled, but the male hopped with insolence almost to the man's face before it too flew away. A while later the goldfinches came to the ditch and they pecked at the foxtail seeds. They clawed at the weeds and they ate and left.

The man prayed. He tried to remember some of the prayers he'd learned long before, but even the common prayer that began with "Our Father" did not come back to him, and he said to himself, dear god, dear god, bring me water, let it rain. He heard himself murmuring, highpitched and laboring, and he said, let the others find me. Let me have water, god.

When he looked again, the sun had visibly lowered, but it was no cooler. He thought perhaps he might have slept, for his head was clearer and he remembered many things. His legs did not pain so badly and he could actually raise himself on his elbow without the pain in his chest preventing it. The puddle of gasoline was still there beside him, and it was widening, and he noticed a different coloration, that the liquid was redder and thicker, and it came to him that he was bleeding, that he had been losing that steady trickle of blood all day and his blood and the gasoline were collecting there in front of him.

He was enraged suddenly, and he wanted to weep in his terrible anger. He pressed with all his strength against the hot wheel of the tractor, but nothing moved. He struck at the red steel of the tractor, and the metal was too hot to touch. The metal was foreign and alien there, burning and glistening, and there he was, he thought in his fury, caught beneath the machine, pinned by the hot, unwholesome metal into the earth, and he could not do anything at all. He beat at the metal until his hands began to bleed again, and it was no use. The hot steel of the tractor was shiny and undented.

The man cursed the machine. The tractor was an enemy to him, he thought, it had thrown him and trapped him, and it would not help him. It had been the tool to say, I give thee death. It had conspired to crush him, it and the sun. And yet, he thought, when the ineffectual struggle was finished, when he lay back again, and yet, the machine was only part of it, for the hostile earth, the sliding bank and the hard, pebbly wash pinned him there, too, and there was the hostile sun, and the blue-burner sky. He was a fool, he thought, there was nothing hostile there, nothing had conspired against him, the world was unchanged. There was really no concern with these things around him, with these things that led him to death, there was only disconcern and utter detachment. He was the alien, the hostile one, there. The land and the things that grew from the land, and the metal sky and the hot sun, and even the machine, fashioned by hands not unlike his, none of them had any concern, and even though he was wedded to that soil, pinned by the earth and the machine, and his blood mixed with the blood of the tractor, he had no connection with anything there. The units were detached; he was alien; he was alone. And he would die as he had lived. It was a terrible realization.

He felt the warm rubber tire, the same tire that pinned him there. The tractor will be all right again, he thought, they will lift the machine and drain it and clean it thoroughly and fill it with fuel and it will run as well as ever; life is not a part of it, it cannot be crushed. He remembered the pride he had had with it, and how he had loved to run this tractor and how he had talked of the work it could do, and how things were better because of this machine. And now only the machine would ever be good again, even if they now lay dead like this together, and the blood ran out of them both and mixed in the gravel beside them.

He turned his face away from the tractor. The sun beat down. The butterflies swarmed, the birds fought and screamed, the breeze touched the languid treetops.

The sun had set itself on the rim of the ditch when the deerflies struck him. They came buzzing suddenly and they tangled in his hair and found his ears to burrow into and they struggled into his nostrils and bit sharply and angrily. The man moved his hands feebly against the flies. He had lost all of his strength, he thought, and then he remembered the bloating, fly-infested bodies of animals he had seen dead in fields, and how the maggots were working almost before the carcass was cool. He thought how it would be to find him like that, green and with the worms lacerating his face, and he fought against the flies, but they were inexorable and angry. The man became furious too, and he struck at them, and then he dug at the dirt and he covered his skin and his head with dust and crumbs of dirt. The flies persisted, but the man covered himself finally, and he lay beneath the gentle and cool layer of dust, with his hand over his nostrils, and the flies left gradually, and he was alone again.

The sun watched him lingeringly and moved with slowness beyond the edge of the bank. It was cool then, suddenly. The evening clouds came up, with the color of wine. The birds shrilled and worked high after mosquitoes. The butterflies were gone; they had gone with the sun. And there was the scurry of small animals in the weeds.

The flakes in his skull were falling rapidly now, he thought, there was no feeling in him anymore, it was as if the weight of the tractor was already off him, as if there was no machine, no life, no light, nothing around him; the world was settling in his flaking-off brain.

There was a padding sound near him and he saw the lean coyote slip along the bed of the ditch, and the coyote sniffed at the straw hat and it turned the hat, and the light wind rolled the hat very near the man, almost to his head. The coyote saw the man then and it came up, sniffing gingerly. The coyote had eyes that were yellow-green and the eyes burned in the darkness like oil, and the animal came to sniff at the dust-covered and swollen strangeness, and it brought its wet nostrils to within an inch of the man's. The coyote backed away and it began to pant lightly, and it scratched itself, leisurely, and then its head came up, alert, and the animal turned and slipped away, without sound.

The man thought he heard voices and shouts and footsteps and he looked up. No, he had been dreaming, he thought, and he turned his body quite easily. He recalled the yellow-green eyes, like fire, and he wondered if he had dreamed that too. His hand flung out and he touched moisture, and his mouth gagged after water, and it took him a thrilling instant to realize it was the gasoline puddle beside him. It was thick now, and coarse with blood.

The night came on blackly, the stars were out, and the locusts and crickets buzzed with violence near beside him. The moon rose above the ditch, and it was enormous and flattened and gold.

The eyes and the mouth of it were agonized and lamenting. The man was glad when he saw the moon. The moon is my sister, he thought. The flakes within his skull were falling upon his eyes, and he thought of someone or something bringing him water. Overhead, the wind-swayed willows made scratches against the terrible moon.

The Quick and the Dead

I was looking for stray calves that wind-whipped, violently cold morning. The cattle were in the yards, but there were two missing and so I went out across the stubble fields to look for them, while my brother, who owned that farm, finished the morning work. The snow was deep in the fields; it had started to snow lightly during the afternoon of the previous day, in flurries at first, and during the night it had come heavily, with a high wind, and it was drifted and banked with an ice-hard covering.

The day was clear, with an icicle-blue clearness, and the frigid sun huddled not far above the horizon, surrounded in its rainbow of sun dogs. At the hilltop, a half-mile from the place, the wind was like frozen stilettos in my eyes and on my face and it took my breath away. The wind howled fiercely out of the northwest, carrying the snow and the cold with it. I was dressed warmly, wrapped in sheepskin to my eyes, but the cold was still vicious. The hill was long, dividing the field into two nearly equal halves, and the half I crossed to took up a quarter-section of land itself. The field had once been an entire farm, but the farmstead now lay abandoned and gray, surrounded by the thistle-like trees in one corner of the land, not far from the schoolhouse, which too had long since been boarded-up and abandoned.

Across the long hollow, beside the schoolhouse, I saw a patch of green, metallic and shiny, and there were drifts all around the gray building. It was too cold to think well, and the oddness of that bright color made no impression on me at first. I saw the two calves huddled in a hollow, under the lip of a snow bank, not far away, and I ran down there, and I pulled the calves up roughly, because I knew their lives depended on moving quickly. They were without energy and I pushed them along ahead of me to the hilltop, slapping them with my hands, and they huddled their frail backs with the wind and finally they began to scamper off towards the place.

I wondered at the greenness, and I looked across the long valley at the schoolhouse. It was difficult to see against that piercing glare of the sun on the glazed white snow and against the wind. The green metal was there, obliterated at moments by the blowing snow. It was a fallen shutter, I thought at first, but I knew there were no metal shutters there, and no signs blown in on that isolated road and by that building. I knew I would have to go down there.

It was hard going, and the hollow was drifted up, and I kept breaking through the crust of the snow. I came up from the hollow, sinking in the deep snow and struggling through it, and the wind was vicious, and the cold sank into me, like fangs. I crossed the bedraggled schoolyard fence. There had once been many trees around the schoolhouse, but only grass and weeds grew there anymore, and there were two old box elder trees, near dying, and two already dead and fallen over, and one small evergreen, and a covey of plum brush which nothing could kill. The building itself was ratty and tattered, and some of the shingles had come off and the boards hung loosely from the black windows. The snow was drifted deeply around the schoolhouse, and the roof was swept clear by the wind.

I circled the building warily, for even in my chilled mind I was a little afraid. It was as I had guessed; there was no shutter there, no sign blown down. A car was parked beside the building, out of the northwest wind, and the snow had blown in, drifting over the front of the car. It was the green metal side of the automobile that I had seen from the hilltop. I hesitated, and then I kicked through the deep snow to the car. The front of the car and the side of it near the building were covered over with hard but fragile-looking little curlicues of wind-shaped snow. The snow was as clean and brilliant white as a wedding veil. The windows of the car were frosted over from the inside, and I knew that meant that someone had been within the car when it was freezing out, and the moisture had condensed and frozen on the windows. I was frightened, and I slapped my mittened hands together. I knew the car had not been there the previous evening, for the snow had only begun then, and I had brought the tractor down across the stubble, herding the cattle back to the barns, and nothing had been there. The car had come in the night, when the wind was still blowing the dirt country road clear. Perhaps the people in the car had set out on foot, I thought; I hoped they had, for there was nothing that could live long in that weather.

I rubbed the glass gingerly, but the frost was inside, I remembered stupidly, and then, through the fragile, laced frost at the edges of the glass, I saw the clump on the front seat, and I knew then, even in my frozen brain, what had happened. I shouted and I beat upon the window. I tried the door but it was locked. Nothing moved.

I wore heavy leather mittens and I hit the window once, twice, three times, and the window smashed, shattering glass and the window frost into the car, and I reached in and opened the door.

A man and a woman were on the front seat and they were in an embrace, and they were dead. A blanket was pulled up over part of them. There was a quick coldness in my belly and I was afraid I would vomit, but I did not. I did not look again at them, then. I pulled the blanket farther over them both, hiding the heads, and then I heard the little buzzing sound. The ignition was on. I reached in carefully, over the two, not touching them, and turned the keys off. They had come there in the night, I thought, and because it was cold they had left the motor and the heater run, and the gas had been drawn in and the odorless monoxide covered and suffocated them, before the storm and the cold had penetrated the car. The engine had run until all the gasoline was gone.

I was trembling and I closed the door and took a few steps away, and I could not think of anything, and then I was driven back to the car because I could not believe it. It was as if I had fallen somewhere in that bitter cold and was freezing to death and I was dreaming it all. I opened the door once more. They were there, and I knew them. The woman was Mathilda Heron, the wife of a farmer who lived not far away, and the man was Conrad Wenzel, a young man not yet thirty, who was new in the town and who was a teacher in the junior high school.

I slammed the door hard and I ran and the wind lashed, prickly and cold, against the backs of my legs, and even though I fell several times in that deep and treacherous snow, I did not stop running. The hill was long, and the ice-air clutched at my lungs, and each breath became a cold and bitter agony, like teeth clamped into my chest, but I could not stop running.

My brother was waiting for me and he was standing in the warmth where the cattle were feeding, and I leaned, sweating and cold, against the board fence, and I told him what I had seen.

He blinked and he struck his forehead with his hand and asked me twice if I was sure, and I nodded each time. He swore and shook his head and said the sheriff would have to be called.

"The sheriff will have to come quickly," I said.

"Why?" my brother asked. "They won't move from the car."

"They don't matter," I said. "Everybody else will find out if it isn't done quietly and quickly."

My brother shrugged his shoulders, and he looked at me as if to ask what else we could do. It was not our affair, and there was nothing either of us could do about it.

"Yes, all right," I said. "Call the sheriff."

We went up to the house where it was warm, and my brother placed the call, and while he waited for the sheriff to come to the phone, we looked at each other, and we both knew what it meant in that country, with the party lines and all the men sitting at home in front of their stoves, gathering reports from their telephone-listening wives. My brother tried to tell the sheriff to simply come out, but the sheriff, too, could see the weather; and it was eighteen miles from the county seat to our place, and so finally my brother had to tell him angrily that there were two dead people in a car, and the sheriff asked him if he knew who they were, and my brother said "no," and hung up. We knew then that the whole neighborhood, the whole town, would know within a matter of hours, would hungrily feed on the details, in the way that starved cats pull at the entrails of fish until they had them all.

My brother swore shortly, surprising his wife.

We could hear the phone ringing and my brother's wife answering it before we got out the door; the neighbors were beginning to call.

We took the tractor, and axes to cut wood for a fire, and some gasoline in case the car could be moved, and two old blankets. The tractor had chains and was powerful and it did not have trouble with the drifts. We went up over the hill, the way I had come, for it was the shortest way. We pulled the fence down at the schoolhouse yard and drove the tractor up beside the car. The blowing snow was filtering in upon the two people now, and they were partly frozen; we could tell that by the strange, hardened white color of the flesh of them.

I attacked some fallen branches with the axe and chopped out some firewood, and I built a fire in a small bare spot, not far from the car. I pulled down some of the dry boards that had been used to cover the schoolhouse windows, and in a short while there was a good blaze going.

My brother looked at the bodies and he came over to the fire, and we talked about them.

When the farm a quarter-mile to the south had been operating, the road along there had been in use, and the country schoolhouse was used, too, a few years before, but with the enlarging of our farm and the other farms around there and the hard-surfacing of the county road a half-mile to the south, the country road and the school had no purpose, and both were abandoned. The road and the schoolhouse yard were used lavishly in the summer times by high school lovers. Many times, late in the evening, while at work in the fields, we had seen the cars parked in the same place where this green car stood. It was a favorite place, near enough to town, and there was no traffic, and it had opportunity and darkness. And these two had come here in the dead of winter, for their privacy, their opportunity to make love without anyone knowing, for they were both married, and each of them had children. It was a good place for lovers, and these, too, would have escaped without notice, but for the treachery of the snow and the cold.

My brother and I went to see if the car could be moved, but the drifts were packed and hard, and it was too viciously cold, and we returned to the fire. I thought of the woman, Mathilda Heron, and of her husband, Rudy Heron, and what kind of man he was, and I said, "We should move them out of the car at least. If Rudy comes down here, if he hears about it, there will be trouble."

My brother nodded, but he hesitated when I opened the door of the car. The bodies were wound in the blanket, and to move them out and separate them, we would have to lift them out after the blanket was taken off. My brother looked at the woman's face, and he would not touch them, although I knew he was very tough about seeing things dead, and he was three years older than I and had had more experience. I could not move them alone, and I did not ask him again to help. The woman did something to my brother, I could see by his face.

My brother had not been married long, and he had told me a long time before about the woman, Mathilda Heron, and how she used to get drunk sometimes in the bars in town, and how the men could talk easily to her, and she loved the attention of men, and they could take her out to the country, if the men pleased her, and most of them did. My brother had been one of these men, a year or so before, and I knew he was thinking about her. There was a gentleness in his eyes, and I knew he was thinking that even though she may have been too free, perhaps even a whore, she had done no harm to him, or to any of the other men.

The woman's husband, Rudy Heron, was intensely jealous of her, and he used to get drunk, and try to follow her, and he swore he would kill anybody with her, but everybody laughed at him behind his back and thought him to be a fool, because he could not adequately keep his woman. The longer it carried on, the worse his jealousy became, and the louder his talk, and the drunker he was on those hot and violent evenings, and then even he knew he could not take her home as he should, or follow her, all he could do was slump over the bar and mutter and rage to himself.

Mathilda Heron was a pretty woman, I remembered. She had

clear, clean skin, and a very large bosom, which, haltered and proper, she liked to thrust before the eyes of the men, and she had bright, very alive, brown eyes, and light-brown hair, and nice enough legs, with full, smooth calves, in spite of the four children she had borne. Even those four young children could not dissuade the woman, and one could see in her eyes her tigerish wants, and her husband was not her man.

The schoolteacher we knew only vaguely. I had seen Conrad Wenzel a few times in town, and he was a slender, cleanly handsome man. He was always neat and well-dressed, I remembered, as if he had come directly from a shower, and he had a ready smile, and I vaguely remembered his wife beside him on the street, and a child or two. His wife was dark-haired and pleasant, and slender, and I did not know her further than that.

Then they started coming, the neighbors. They came over the hill on their tractors, following the tracks we had made. They had heard about it by the telephone, and now they came, like vultures, to look upon the bodies. I said what I thought to my brother, and he shrugged his shoulders and said, "Ah, we probably would be doing the same thing if somebody else found them."

"But it's different," I said. "It makes it our responsibility this way, because we found them."

"What do you mean?" he asked.

"The other people," I said.

"I don't know what we've got to do with them," he said.

The farmers arrived; there was Kamrad and Heintzelman and Anderson, and the first two were big and powerful Dutchmen, and Anderson was a thin Swede, and they were all bundled thickly against the weather. They climbed off their tractors and went to the car and looked, and they were astonished, except for Anderson who had to lift the blanket to peer more closely, and he sucked between his teeth all the while he looked.

The men came to the fire, and they nodded at us. "Does Rudy Heron know?" Heintzelman asked.

My brother and I shook our heads negatively.

"We better move them out of there," I said. No one replied and no one moved.

"I took a load of cobs over to Rudy's place this morning," Anderson said in that high-pitched, still-Swedish voice of his. He had been born in this country, but he had taken the accent from his father. "Rudy didn't say anything about his wife not being there, at home. I did think it funny he didn't take me in the house to get warm."

"How could he say anything about his wife not being home?" my brother asked, slowly and mildly. "Would anybody say anything if his wife was gone, and hadn't come home all night?"

"Rudy's awful jealous of her," Kamrad said.

"He had a reason to be jealous this time," Anderson said, with his high-pitched giggle. He looked around at them, as if hoping someone else would giggle, too.

The men looked at the car, and knelt beside the fire and chipped at the wood and threw some sticks into the fire, and looked at the car again, and hoped it would not be there.

"I wish that sheriff would get here," my brother said.

That is what they all want, I thought. They wanted the sheriff to come, and take it all off their hands, so they could go home and not think about it anymore.

"Rudy Heron's going to come down here," I said. "He'll hear about it and he'll come down here, and it won't be good."

"What can we do about it?" Heintzelman asked.

Anderson gave his high-pitched laugh. "Ya, what can we do? We can't stop him if he wants to come and look at his wife." He looked around at the others.

"We better pull them out of the car and wrap them up separately, here on the snow," I said.

"No, you better not do that," Anderson said. "The sheriff might not like that, when he gets here. He wants to see them like they are."

I did not like Anderson. He could incense me quickly. "Nobody has to see them like that, the sheriff or Rudy Heron or anybody else."

"You could get into trouble touching them," Anderson said. "They got to make an investigation. You'd be changing things, and you might get arrested."

"We've got to do something," I said, looking first at Anderson, and then at the other men, too, for I could tell they nearly agreed with him. They looked into the fire, and not at me. "What about if Rudy Heron comes here? It's the man's wife," I went on loudly, almost shouting at them, at these married men. "The woman's dead. He can know that, but to see her this way . . . We've got to do something."

"Ach, everybody knows what kind of woman she was," Anderson said.

I was suddenly angry, and I jumped up and went around the fire and put myself in front of Anderson. "Who knows?" I shouted into his face. Anderson backed away from me and pointed at the car. "You want to tell everybody, don't you?" I went on. "You don't give a damn if everybody talks, and the kids and the husband and wife of those two hear about it the rest of their lives. You want to bring Rudy Heron and the whole goddamn neighborhood down here to look at them, don't you?"

"That's the way they died," Anderson said.

I felt my shoulder move, wanting to hit him, but I did not. I dropped my hands and turned away from him. They were all afraid to do anything, afraid of any kind of action or involvement. Anderson, the men, even my brother wanted to treat it as if it did not really concern them. They did not want to protect the other people; they did not care.

"Do you have to get so mad all the time?" my brother asked. He was always the cooler one of us.

"They're dead," I said. "Let them be dead. Who gives a damn now what they were doing. But nobody else needs to know, and nobody needs to get hurt, their kids or anybody else." I went by the men, one by one, and looked at them. "I'll move them myself," I said.

"I'll help you," Heintzelman said finally.

Heintzelman and I went to the car, but no one else would help. The bodies were hard as steel and we had a difficult time of it. We found the underclothing of the two, but the pieces were wet and had frozen and even after holding the clothing above the fire and thawing them we could not put them on because of the positions of the bodies. We buttoned them up as well as we could. We were working quickly, but there was nothing we could do, and when we heard the sound of the tractors coming over the hill, we wrapped the bodies quickly in the blankets and laid them in the snow, between the car and the fire.

It was Mellon and Orth and Tangro, farmers in the neighborhood, who came on the tractors, and Orth had brought his fourteen-year-old son along.

"Look what they're bringing," I said loudly. "A boy, a kid. Next it'll be their wives and all their kids, and then we can all sit down here and have a goddamn picnic."

"The boy is old enough," my brother said. "What's wrong with him coming?"

"Old enough?" I said. "Is that why you and everybody else here turned pale when you saw what was in the car? Sure, let the boy come. That's fine. Let's have a big exhibition because we're all so pure, and somebody else got caught. Let's invite everybody down here to look at somebody else's exposed sin." I looked directly into my brother's eyes. "We're all pretty pure, aren't we?" I said.

He rubbed his forehead and almost wearily turned away from me. "Why did you bring the boy?" my brother asked Orth, when the tractors came up.

Orth was taken aback. His mouth opened to speak, but he said nothing, and then he laughed, tittering and confused, for he was surprised at my brother talking like that. "The boy's old enough," he said finally.

"Send him home," my brother said sharply. The boy looked open-mouthed at my brother and then at his father.

"What is it?" the father asked. "Who's dead?"

"Send the kid home," I said.

"Ya, ya," Heintzelman said slowly. "Send him home."

Orth told the unwilling boy to take the tractor and leave.

When the boy was gone, the men came up and looked at the bodies and one of the men whistled and they came to the fire, sober-faced.

Mellon stood shivering and rubbing his hands. "It's cold down here," he said, and I knew he wanted to talk about something other than the two dead people.

It was bitter cold, and the wind hurtled in across the treeless fields to the west, and the tiny ice-crystals of snow were like sand.

"They're pretty warm, I bet, shoveling coal in hell," Anderson said, and he gave a short laugh, like a stuttering cough. He nudged Mellon and said, "Ach, they died happy," in his sniggering, rotten voice.

"Snicker, you dumb son of a bitch," I said. I wanted to put my hands on his scrawny rooster's neck and strangle him.

"What you say to me?" he said. "I hit you if you say that to me."

I stood up from the place where I'd been squatting beside the fire, and I stepped in front of Anderson, and I put my face an inch from his. "Hit me then, and I'll break your neck and send you straight to hell, too, you dumb Swede Lutheran bastard." We went to the same church, so I knew I could talk to him that way with impunity.

Anderson was frightened and he stood back. He shrugged his shoulders to the others, as if it was I that had gone mad.

"What's wrong with you?" my brother asked me.

"He thinks this is all funny," I said, "the way we all sit around here not doing anything, knowing that somebody will get hurt from it. He thinks it's a joke if people have to suffer. Look at his face. You can see what the simple fool is thinking in his dumb face."

"You better calm down," my brother said.

"I'd like to," I said. "Two people are dead, but that isn't enough. Everybody has to know about it, and they have to get hurt, because a stupid dumb hypocrite like that stands around and snickers. He can hardly wait to get out of here so he can tell about it. He wants to see the other people hurt and in trouble." I was shouting, and I went around the fire from the men and wouldn't talk to them.

We heard the tractor coming a little later, and the sound of it was from a different direction, and we all stood to look, and the tractor came from the south, up from the cleared, hard-surface road. The tractor plowed and bucked against the hard, heavy drifts, but still it came on, furiously. There was a little wagon, more nearly a cart, only a sawedoff box over four tiny wheels, trailing the tractor, and the cart bounced and slid from side to side on that rough road. It was Rudy Heron.

We could see the wrapped, small heads moving with the hard movements of the cart.

"He brought the kids along," my brother and I said together, with the same thought and in the same astounded and awful voice. Heintzelman groaned, and suddenly it was as if all the men there knew of our relationship to the two dead people; even Anderson was silent. We all moved together then, and made a half-circle around the bodies and waited for Heron.

The tractor had chains and even then it was difficult to steer, we could see that, and Rudy was holding the wheel of the tractor with savage concentration, and the cart behind lurched and swayed. The heads of the children kept bobbing up and down and they tried to hold on to the board sides.

The tractor was there, and Rudy Heron left it running wide-open, very loudly, and he jumped down and walked over to us, and in the cart the children peeped over the edge at their father and us.

"Is my wife here?" Rudy asked, striding towards us. He was a slightly built man, dark-faced, and his jaw and face were long and narrow, and he had not shaved, and the thin sliver of a scar on the tip of his chin was very white against his blue-black face. His eyes were small and yellowish and glittering, unalive, like the eyes I had seen in dead animals.

"Is my wife here?" he asked loudly, again, and he came on into our midst.

"She's here," my brother said, holding his arm out and stopping Heron. Heron struck at my brother's arm, but my brother turned with him, stepping back, but still between him and the bodies.

Heron looked at my brother's face, and then he seemed to get control of himself, and he said, "I want to see my wife. Which one is she?"

"Here," my brother said. He backed away from Heron, and he knelt and pulled the blanket down an inch or two to expose the upper part of the dead woman's face.

Heron looked at her, and he rubbed his beard and his eyes, and we thought he might be crying, but then he asked, "Who was she with?" He turned to look at the ashen-faced and sober men. "Who?" No one said anything.

Heron's eyes burned us one by one. "Who?"

"Conrad Wenzel," Heintzelman said, coughing out the name. "He must have been bringing her home, and they made a wrong turn, got lost, and thought this was a farm or something. Probably got stuck." Heintzelman was speaking rapidly, but his voice gradually became less and less firm. "It was easy for Wenzel to get lost. He's not from around here, you know." His voice trailed off.

"I know," Heron shouted. "I know Wenzel. Come mooning around my wife. I seen what was going on." He looked at the woman's face. "Who found them?" he asked.

"I did," I said.

"And how was they? What was they doing?"

"Sitting," I said. "Sitting in the front seat, dead. It was the gas from the engine . . ."

"Sitting! Hah! Sitting!" Heron leapt suddenly at the blanket-covered body of the woman and he tore the blanket back, out of my brother's hands, and Heron began to howl, and he laughed and howled, and he fairly leaped around the body, and he turned and bellowed for the children to come there and look at their dead mother. "Come," he bellowed, in his strangely deepened and rasping voice. "Look at her, look what she was doing when she died. She's a whore. Look, your mother's a whore. Come look, see what she is." Suddenly he flung the blanket away, and the wind picked it and rolled it, and Heron plunged at the other body, while we stood there, frozen, watching him, and none of us could move. Heron tore that blanket off too. He began to kick the body, hard, with his heavy boots, and he kicked at the groin of the dead man, as if all of the dead man and all of Heron's hate were concentrated there, and Heron was howling and his face was wild and he was frothing at the mouth and the froth froze on his face, like white scars.

My brother caught Heron's arms and pulled him away, but

Heron lunged at my brother and shoved him backwards, over the body of the woman, into the snow. Heron seized one of the sticks I had cut for the fire, and he began to beat on the face and body of the dead man, and the body rolled onto its back and the frozen hands were at its shoulders, supplicating, and the eyes and the mouth were open, and the dead man seemed to be screaming, bleating in agony, but the only sound was the other agony of Heron in his shrieking. Heron slashed and beat with the stick upon the dead body, and the stick made terrible, coldly white, everlasting marks on the frozen flesh, making the peculiar gritting sound like the sound a spoon inserted into a half-frozen box of berries makes, and the marks of the stick would never be erased.

The men stood back in a cluster, horrified, afraid of Heron. Only my brother knew what to do. He came up again, and he spun Heron around and tried to hold him away from the mutilation, but Heron struck my brother on the shoulder with the stick. I moved behind Heron and I jerked his arm behind his back and twisted at the claws of his hand until the stick came free, and I kicked it away, into the fire. Heron twisted loose, and he came towards me, howling everything and nothing. I hit him on the mouth, and his eyes didn't change at all, in spite of the blood in his mouth, and he kept howling and spitting blood. I pulled my arm back quickly and I hit him hard, back-handing him with the hard leather mitten across his face, and the blow made him groan and blink and turn, and I went in quickly and I brought my arm beneath his and twisted him over, and my brother was helping me, and we swung Heron down, crashing him hard against the frozen ground and snow, and his face drove into the packed snow.

I put my knee on him, and I leaned over him and I said, "Come to yourself, man."

It was all out of him then. He lay there, gargling and spitting saliva and blood, and he made biting motions in the snow, and even when I stood up he just lay there, and he was crying, and making noises as a hungry animal makes when it is eating ravenously, and his jaws worked on the snow. It was terrible, listening to him, and all the men were frightened and ashamed, and they wouldn't look at him. We all knew that in a way Heron truly loved the woman, in spite of everything, he did love her, and he was a victim of that, and he hated her, too, and it was something none of us could help him with.

My brother went around Heron and he carefully wrapped the bodies again.

The children had come from the cart and I did not know how long they had been standing there. They had been watching, and their eyes were seared with it all, and they were terrified. There were four children and the oldest was about seven and the youngest about two, and both the oldest and the youngest were girls, and the middle two were boys.

"Why did he bring them?" I said, and I looked again at the man groveling in the snow, and I wanted to drive my boot into his groaning side.

I went around to the children and I brought them up to the fire to warm them and I carefully turned them away so they could not see their father. The children were frightened and quiet, but they kept turning their heads to see the man.

They were terribly cold in that bitter wind, and they had been dressed hurriedly and badly, and the little girl had lost a mitten and her overshoes were on the wrong feet. I rubbed her frigid cheeks and I gave her my large mitten to put on and I tried to play with her, to have her smile, but she would not. She said some words that children say very early and I felt my jaw trembling, and I could not speak at all, and I set her gently on a little log and I took off her overshoes and put them on the right way. I buttoned the other children up properly, and gave my scarf to the older boy, who did not have one. I took the children to the cart again, after they were a little warm, and the oldest girl was crying and looking back at her father, and I could tell in her eyes that she had seen too much, and she would never forget any of it now, none of them would ever forget. It was terrible, that understanding look, that recognition in a child's eyes. When the other children saw their sister crying, they too began to cry. And I thought, we have done this to them, all of this; it was as much our fault as the fault of their father.

I put them on the cart, one by one, and I tried to comfort them, but it was no use. Even in my arms they remembered too well, and they looked past me to see their father and mother. I motioned to my brother, for I couldn't speak, and he brought some blankets from the car, the ones they, the mother and the man, had used to cover themselves, and I wrapped the children warmly. Kamrad came over to drive the children to our place. My brother stood beside me and watched Kamrad and the tractor and the children go, but I could not see them, for my eyes were blinded by that glaring sun and the vivid, hurting snow, and my nose was running, and wetness froze on my cheeks.

I had tried, I thought; feebly and without hope I had tried, and it was not good enough, and I was angry. I slapped my bare hand and my mitten together and I went back to the fire.

"Did you have to bring the children?" I shouted at Heron. "I don't care what happens to you. You can go to hell. But did you have to bring them?"

Heron still lay stretched on the ground, his face in the snow, and the snow around him was pinked by his blood. I beat my hands together, and I remembered it all, especially the children, and I looked at Heron, and I could not contain that feeling any longer. I went over to him and I swore loudly at him and I kicked him hard, very hard, in the side, at the place where the ribs end.

His breath came out of him in a contorted gasp, a kind of bark. I was glad. I wanted to hurt him.

"Get up," I shouted at him. I took his collar and jerked him, when he did not move quickly. Heron braced himself on his hands, and he groaned, and lifted himself painfully. He clutched his side and he stood up and walked feebly and slowly, as if he had become aged and senile in that moment. I followed him, threatening him, and he looked at my coat collar and not into my eyes, and he did not even care then. He would not have cared if I had killed him. He slumped down upon the log where the little girl had sat, and he bent himself at the waist, holding his side and rocking back and forth against the pain, and moaning.

My brother took my arm and pulled me away from Heron. "Let him alone," he said. "He has lost his wife. Let him alone."

"Yes," I said.

I needed to do something, and I got an axe and I chopped a considerable pile of firewood, and I threw all the wood on the fire at once, until there was a very large blaze. I didn't care if the bodies melted and the schoolhouse burned.

We waited forty-five minutes more for the sheriff to arrive and no one said a word in all that time. The only sounds were of my axe and of the snapping fire, and of the wind driving its bitter coldness over us.

The sheriff came in a truck with chains, up the track that Rudy Heron and his tractor had made. He sprang out of the truck before it stopped and he came over to us. He was a spry old man who looked like an insurance salesman, with his smooth and dimpled face and his goldrimmed spectacles. His face was high-colored in the cold, and it was round and pink, like a pale and fat and squashy tomato. He knelt to examine the bodies, and he murmured things to himself and made notes in a pad, and his face remained rosy and calm.

"About the newspapers . . ." my brother said.

"It has to be reported," the sheriff said.

"Just that they were sitting there and they died of monoxide poisoning, and nothing about night," I said. "It happened in broad daylight."

"They've been dead quite a while," the sheriff said. "Late last night, probably." He sucked between his gold teeth. "What is your interest in all this?" he asked me.

"It's not in them; it's the other people," I said.

The sheriff looked at me a moment and then he nodded. "All right," he said. "That's how you found them then?"

"Yes. Just sitting," I said.

"In broad daylight, sitting on a country road, stranded in a blizzard, and the engine was running to keep them warm," the sheriff murmured. He pursed his lips and made some notes in the pad.

"Just like that," I said. It was a foolish attempt, I thought, and hopeless, and everyone would know and talk and snicker, but it made me feel a little better.

The sheriff tried to talk to Heron, but Heron would not say anything at all. He groaned in that steady hurting sing-song way, as he had been for nearly an hour, and his eyes rolled strangely, and he held his side.

Someone told the sheriff that Heron had a sister in Charleston, and the sheriff said that was good, they could take him there, since he was in a bad way.

They loaded the bodies onto the truck, and with the bodies out of sight, and with Heron in the cab with the sheriff, the coldness came on all of us again. We felt the hard wind, and some of the farmers looked at the sun and talked of getting home for dinnertime.

My brother asked me if I wanted to go along to town in the truck, to the undertaker, but I said no.

"We made a mistake," I said. "We should have taken them in by ourselves, before anyone knew about them."

"We might have got into trouble," my brother said. "The sheriff had to be here."

"It was a mistake," I said. "No one should have known about it, especially the children. We did it badly; it was our fault."

"You know how it is in this country. Everyone would have found out and talked about it anyway. We did everything we could do."

"We didn't protect the others," I said. "It was a mistake."

My brother looked at me, and he spread his hands, and I knew that he understood what I was saying. He turned and went to the truck.

"If you see Conrad Wenzel's wife, be careful with her," I said after him. "Don't tell her how it was."

"She will know all about it already," he said. "It will be all right with her anyway. Women are tougher about these things than men."

My brother got into the truck and it turned around and went back up the road. The farmers watched the truck go, and then they got on their tractors and drove up the long hill, to go to their warm houses and their dinners and their talk.

The wind was fierce and the fire had died, and I let the last few logs sizzle against the blowing snow. The car stood beside the building, and the open door was swinging in the wind. The snow drifted into the car, whitely and cleanly. I thought of closing the door, but the window was broken anyway, and the snow could not be kept out. It did not make any difference. The snow and the cold and the wind had killed them, and now it would cover everything, coldly and cleanly and treacherously, and only the cold and falsely clean and treacherous minds of the people would remember it all.

I was alone down there, and I felt the chill of the place, and I wanted to get away. I started the tractor and drove over the fence-line and across the hollow. Behind me, the tracks were filling up with the fine hard crystals, and the fire was out, and the school-yard was twisted and reshaped and very white. It was as if there had never been anyone there, but the wind and the winter snow.

The Witch

Up from the road where they passed they could see the tiny house, gray where the weather struck, surprisingly white in tips beneath the darkened eaves, the house a sudden box on the expanse of land that rode the horizon like a plateau up from the road.

"Who lives there?" one of the twins, the thin-faced one, asked.

"The Widow O'Neill," the old man said. He drove the Model-A Ford of course, the furious-lipped mother on the other front seat, the four brothers in back, Werner the oldest, Walter, and the twins of twelve, Herman, the thin-faced one, and Henry, the round-faced one.

They passed the lane and the old and creased mailbox, the box without name or sign, open to the wind as if nothing had ever been received or expected, the lane width of one car, straight up the low incline, turned sharply up there, ran back of the house, ditch on either side.

"Don't look like anybody lives there," Herman said.

"She's there. Sometimes they don't see her for a month or more," the father said.

"Irish trash," the grim-faced mother said.

"The Nystroms do her farming, don't they?" Werner the old-est said.

"Ya," the father said.

"Boy, I wouldn't go over there for anything," Werner said.

"Why not?" Herman asked, cranking back to watch from the square rear window.

"Shut up. Fool kid's talk," the mother said.

They moved in the barren spring. (The father could not keep a place.) The boys were used to it, were not troubled by the change in schools or the change in bedrooms; the beds were the same. They had an excitement in the discovery of this new place, wandered gladly across its hilly acres in search of the cows at evening, and came to the hill, to the weed-encrusted tumble fence with its old posts made of tree branches and its rusted wire. There at the hilltop they could see the house of the Widow O'Neill, this the reverse side, the dirt road far away now, the lane coming up, turning sharply, the ditches on either side, the gray chicken coop and one other shed, nothing else, no tree, nothing. The tractor of Nystrom buzzed in the field by the road.

Always watching in the marvelous fascination of a different thing, a hope of something mysterious and strange, they looked, turned, looked again, called to the cows, these mongrel cows, roans and brindles, all skinny and mean, headed them back to the place.

On their own side of the fence, there across the far hill in dull placidness they could see the old man and the slow horses barely move along the hillside, the plow leaving a narrow furrow, without sound. The cows clicked home in that spring dust, the fence jumpers wearing their halters of barbed-wire which nevertheless did not keep them in. The cows needed constant watching.

"Let's go up and see the Widow's house, what do you say?" Henry said. He was the heavier, the round-faced one.

Queasy feeling in his belly, a fear he did not like, made Herman, the slender one, avert his face. "All right," he muttered, barely audible.

But milking came and supper and Henry made neither sound nor motion, as if he had forgotten it. Herman wondered why, and was glad they did not go.

It came somewhat later, unexpected.

They kicked up a badger one afternoon and chased the puffing thick creature down to the fence and under it, to its hole in the open field, almost catching up to it.

They scraped at the edge of the hole for a time, knowing it was purposeless. "We'll tell Werner. He'll trap him," Henry said.

The excitement gone, Herman looked down then, down the hill to that quietness where the house stood, intruder in that arid space, the color of dry bark on this northern side where the winter winds could pummel it black, sharp and angular projection with neither tree nor shrub between it and the straight horizon.

"Come on, there's nobody there now," Henry said, still flushed from the rush after the badger.

The afternoon sun was hot (it was May), the oat field they walked on had turned pale, pale green if one looked obliquely and caught the shiver of leaves, but straight down were only the brown clouds.

They walked stiff-legged, carefully. It was easy to begin, Herman thought.

"If someone's there we'll say we're after water," Herman said, liking that slyness of thought.

"There's nobody there, you can see that," Henry said, but with a hesitation in his walk, almost a stumble, that made Herman go first.

They went past the chicken coop. One hen, four chicks scruffing in the dirt, the hen lifting feathers at them when they came too close. They saw the wood lean-to by the house and a cob shed.

"See, there's nobody here," murmured Henry. He went to the window, Herman following, to look in, and then suddenly, hideously, long, lean, dark, black from the doorway quickly noiselessly opened, the figure lifted, pale face, pale hair issuing from the darkness of the house and the darkness of the slender hard body, a ferocious gaggle in the throat, and they sucked in their breaths.

Terrible sound issuing although the words, he knew, were only, "What do you want?" They backed, they fell, rose, and turned and ran and behind them a sound like laughter, a cackle of hell after them, they ran. They ran.

Furtive later. They did not talk of it.

———————◦◆◦———————

They went visiting at times in the evening, the walk up the narrow road to the hilltop to see·Nystrom, old grizzled farmer with big ears and a fat wife and two big-eared sons and two fat daughters. They talked, the women in the house, the men (and boys) outside. Nystrom had a tractor and owned his farm; the old man was obviously impressed, for Nystrom was so common a man, would talk to anyone, not high-toned at all.

"You do the work for the Widow?" the old man asked in the course of the conversation, out sitting on the wooden planking by the pump.

Herman came closer to them at that, listened carefully, pretending to work at the locust tree pod with his fingers.

Yes, Nystrom said, for a share of the crop.

"Funny for a woman to stay there all alone and not move to town."

Guess she likes it that way, Nystrom said. She had talked of going back to Ireland. Had some relatives there, she said.

"Must be a funny one to always be alone in a shanty like that."

Oh, they tell lots of stories about her, the queer things she does, Nystrom said with a nod of his big head. As for him, he saw her only once in a while, sometimes not for months, but she seemed all right to him. Her cousins came sometimes to see her, and the Liles took her to Martinsburg to buy things. She was always friendly to him. Too bad she was alone all the time, but it seemed that was the way she wanted it.

"I saw her once, when I was out getting cows," Henry said suddenly, with bravery to speak out to his elders," and she was real nice."

Herman listened with a horror at his brother, that he should lie in his teeth like that, trying to pretend something he knew not to be true so that they, their elders, would listen to him and think him knowledgeable, and so that everyone would think he liked the woman. Herman was appalled and could not hide it, and did not try to hide it. There was some enormous deceit here that he could not abide; had his brother, twin brother, forgotten the terror of that afternoon moment, the blind and choking fear that had laid itself on their throats so that they could not speak of it, even to each other? How could he dispel so easily that awareness of a greater evil, so surely felt that terrible afternoon? Ah, he lied, he lied.

When they came to walk home, Henry tried to walk beside him but Herman punched him on the arm and they nearly had a fight, the mother accusing Herman of starting it, lunging for him to slap him, but he was too quick, and able in the openness of the space to dodge her.

"I'll get you yet, you little devil," the mother said. "You just wait. I hope he beats you up."

He fell back, did not answer. Fear of the iron-handed parents held him. She hoped the twin would beat him up; that would be the day. He lagged behind, by himself scuffing in the dirt in the moonlit darkness.

From that time on he went alone, trailing the gaunt cows through the pasture, studying through the tumbleweed and burdock litter along the fence the gray house.

He saw her one day in the doorway. And she saw him. He did not move, thought it pointless to try to hide—he was on his own side of the fence—and she stood motionless far down there looking in his direction for a long time, fixed steady, as if casting spells. He was not afraid.

Nor was he afraid when the clouds built up in the early summer afternoons like a massive black brain of darkness, fissured, convoluted, and the heavens roiled, and the whirlwinds coiled like snakes across the patches of the Widow O'Neill. From the brush along the fences, he, unconcerned, almost, gathered blackberries and half-ripened plums where the worms had come and made them turn ripe too soon, an unnatural ripeness, the green side picked with holes, oozing bright juice, hardened and tight, and the other side turned purple-red where he nibbled delicately, with care. The storms did not frighten him, made him shiver a little at the way the clouds mounted powerful as the earth, the lightning snapped downward, tracing branches, stinging white against the black and hollow-looking clouds.

Then he turned the cows home, judging the movement of the storm expertly, timing it even as he ate carefully around the worm lodgement in the plums, brought the cows up to the shelter of the old gray shed just as the first wind and heavy thudding raindrops hit.

The weather passed, the new days sparkled dry, too dry, too much dust, the land too feeble for anything but sunflowers and cockleburs.

She went away one day, came out, closed the door and walked down the lane, tall figure, angular, sharp as a nose, darkly dressed, gray-black skirt, black hat, not walking so much as sweeping along for he could not see the lower third of her from over the stunted sweet clover by the fence. She waited a long time at the mailbox and then the Liles came by in the old Chevy and picked her up.

He went down through the clover patch (the nurse crop of oats had been strangled already) zig-zagging a little almost unconsciously for he knew how the clover could lie over and leave a distinct track. At the chicken coop there was the old hen and two half-feathered chicks. Two gone, he thought.

The air was motionless, entirely. He waited, conscious suddenly of the totality of silence, held his breath and listened, not even the murmur of flies. It was as if he were on another planet, divorced from everything he knew. The hot afternoon burned without sound, without motion. Even the chickens spread their drooping wings in the tiny shade, their beaks locked open, only their throats working.

He had one weak urge to shout, to interrupt that silence, change it somehow, to powerfully alter for a moment this quiet deadness, but the wish boiled off, leaving him impotent and hot.

In darkness of the lean-to beside the house a glimmer of yellow-greenish light, opening, shut. The boy backed away, moving he realized even then with a drugged sluggishness that he would remember, came forward a step, forced himself forward. The oil eyes watched him from under there, open, shut, with a slow mysteriousness as if too under a spell. A cat. He reached in, felt the fur, hand fastened on the acquiescent neck, lifted the cat out, neither cat nor kitten, halfway between, gray, color of ashes, brought it to his curved arm. It sat calmly, turned its head a little.

"Where did you get that?" the mother asked in the evening when he came up from the barn.

"I found it in the pasture," he said.

"Oh, I don't like cats around," she said.

"It'll catch mice," he said.

"See that it stays outside," she threatened.

That determined him. He snuck it in, put it in a box by his screenless window, so that it could go in and out.

On the hot nights he could hear its passage, and sometimes if he awoke he could see the slivers of eyes in the darkness, opening, closing, slowly, very slowly, giving him a peculiar chill.

Perhaps he would have been startled, even afraid, if he had not always been pleased, when thinking of it, at defying his mother's command. The cat was there, inside the house, as he wished.

In the daytime it disappeared, where to he did not know. Saw it from time to time beneath the porch or in the loft of the barn, but usually not at all.

He went regularly to his duty of keeping his eye on the cows. The afternoons swooned with heat. The sun sat in its haze, too bright to look at. His short shadow was noiseless as he, through the thickets by the dry dead stream, through the powdery dust on the path the cows took. The milkweed that he touched filtered pollen upon his hands, the feeble tree-branch posts leaned, drowsed in drunken posture held up by the rusted wires. The cows baked beneath a cottonwood's shade, lashing flies, eyes closed, stomping hoofs against the flies, choking on cuds.

He could hear the sound and he shivered, truly shivered, skin cold as touching a sweating arm. She was singing. Words too distant for him to understand, high-pitched, cracking almost. Nothing musical, even he who knew nothing of music but a few hymns and the schoolroom mutterings to the teacher's piano, knew that this tuneless screeching was a following of some melody he did not know.

He peeped past a post, looked between bunches of sweet clover, yellow blossoms wilted in the motionless heat. He went on his hands and knees, the pollen falling on him, careful not to move the bunches if he could, no wind, no other motion than himself.

She had stopped singing. He waited, looking through the great bunches of clover, webbed and tight and defensive. He was no more than forty feet from the little shanty, the weathered boards stiff and black. Shrilly she started again; a yelp, shriek of sound, stopped again. Language unknown to him.

She came through the doorway, opening into darkness, her movement sending him into a tight, sprung posture, holding all breath, feeling ooze of sweat from his face. She dumped a pan of something, potato peelings, whatever, the one hen came to peck, and one cat too, his cat he believed. And looked again at her. Amazed at how old she seemed, white hair he had only slightly noticed that one time he'd seen her, hair undone, wisps of white down her face as if a white liquid poured over her head, congealed there. Wrinkled, wrung face, pinched mouth. Same angular body, long, long, rising up.

She sang, stood there and shrieked sounds, six or seven words he did not understand, popped the bottom of the dishpan with her hand, freeing the last peel or two, went in again, was silent.

The boy watched the cat glide up, lift one forepaw, sniff at the peelings, sit down, lick itself. His own cat, he believed, although he could not be certain, believed it was his, in that heat nothing registering right, all uncertain for him like unsteady imaginings or dreams.

He went the way he had come.

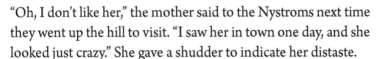

"Oh, I don't like her," the mother said to the Nystroms next time they went up the hill to visit. "I saw her in town one day, and she looked just crazy." She gave a shudder to indicate her distaste.

"She goes in with the Liles," old man Nystrom said, waggling his big head. "They say sometimes her bag of groceries is as big as a candy sack."

"Funny one," Nystrom's wife said. "Always acted strange. I went over there once and she wouldn't even let me in the house."

"Na," the mother said.

"Some say she's done peculiar things."

"I've heard her sing," old man Nystrom said.

"Sing!" the mother cried.

The big man grinned. Yellow, crooked teeth. Big mean blue eyes. "Oh ya, sometimes the whole day through. I've heard her when I stopped the tractor."

"And there are times when she's not around for months," the oldest son said.

"Oh ya, that too," Nystrom said.

"They say she's a witch," Nystrom 's second son said.

They all laughed at that.

Mrs. Nystrom the loudest. "Kept my kids scared for years, telling about the Widow. They would sure mind then."

The mother hissed with laughter.

"Ya, she's kept the kids toeing the line for years over that. Only way they go over there is on a tractor," old Nystrom said.

"Wouldn't catch me gettin offen it neither," the older son said, sucking in his nostril and giggling.

"She is a sight to see sometimes, although some say she was a pretty woman years back," Mrs. Nystrom said. "She's not a witch. Isn't any such thing."

"Shoulda told us that years before," the oldest son said, whickering.

"Let's see, what you need to be a witch?" Nystrom asked. "Pin cushion, baby fat, and a fire. And a . . . a cat. Yeh?"

"Well, I'd never make a witch," the mother said, tee-heeing. "A pin cushion gets too dirty, so I use a box, and I just hate cats."

A pause and old man Nystrom made profound nods of his head, his eyes squinting. "Oh, the Widow's all right, I guess. Never bothered anybody."

No, no, the boy thought, he knew that was not true. All had been planned, all had been figured in that terrible awareness of *him*, he himself, Herman, always that, she knowing of *him* even when singing, walking the lane to await the Liles, always she had known he was there, precisely where and how and when, through the cat awareness of him, surety of *him*, he knowing it now, at last with absolute certitude, nothing on her mind but *him*, she obsessed with *him*, sent the cat to watch *him*, lay in wait to catch *him*. He could feel it on him, like a massive weight, hot, overwhelming.

Old man Nystrom winked profoundly, waggled his big head. "Looka the boy taking it all in," nodding at Herman, the boy's eyes huge, concentrated and dark.

They laughed again, all of them, turning to look at him.

The mother tsutted her tongue and tee-heed. "He's swallowing it whole, it looks like."

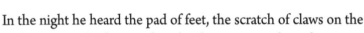

In the night he heard the pad of feet, the scratch of claws on the wall. He sat up in the cot where he slept, saw out there the mysterious moonlight, the breathless night, the shadows, gray and grayer, and near him, here in the very room the slight mew of sound.

"Get out," he whispered, gargle and screech in the back of his throat. "Get out." Thought he saw the blur of gray shadow through the open window.

He saw her in the barn, the cat, in the loft, wilder now, looking at him, not responding to his cold looks and brief entreaties. Or in the large garden, moving delicately as a shadow in the reaches of the fence, watching him. Always it watching him, its eye upon him. At the shoulder of the henhouse, in the hidden foundation of the granary.

In the night he heard the rustling purr close beside him, flailed up at that sound, his body jerking, he striking the wall with fist and elbow as if an electric probe had nudged him. Saw blurred motion when he came awake, sometimes the oil eye, green, blinking, watching him, the fleet and soundless flight, over the sill. He lay awake for hours sometimes in the hot nights, the moon rising ever later, hearing the creaks on the stairs, the hush of the trees outside, out there, hearing the groan of the planet turning, and out there in the brush beneath the trees the swift and decisive collision of things, brief and sudden battles, rattle of earth, weeds, leaves, and something undone.

He had dreams, the sweat hot on him in the airless cubicle of room. Her face appeared, coming to him as she had that day, the first time, sudden, terrifying, her face moving closer, he seeing more clearly, sharply than he could ever remember, the lined thin face, the swatches of white hair, the eyes blue—that bothered him, the blue eyes, he knowing even in sleep that they should be, must be, bloodshot, red, and terrible. She saying, "What do you want?"

He awoke to the dawn and his private terror, moved preoccupied through vast enmities. His twin brother jeered at him for not getting to go along to Martinsburg because he had sullenly talked back to his mother over hoeing the garden. He wrestled his brother to the ground in a silent fury, dirtying him good, breaking one lens of his glasses in the scuffle.

His father had followed the mother's charge to beat him. The father had complied with usual rigor.

"Oh, you're a little devil. A little devil," the mother said. And gave him worse names too. "You need a beating every day."

The other two brothers worked in the field. The Model-A sound chuffed off beyond the stark hills.

The heat of the pain was still on his back from the beating.

He found the cat in the pocket of shade behind their henhouse, the eyes nearly closed to the sun, its full-grown body limber, flexed out, the head lifted a little, it accepting the warmth. He got a saucer of the precious milk from the cave where it cooled, cajoled the cat with it, brought the cat forward, drew the gunny sack behind him, waited. The head dipped, the little pink tongue touched at the saucer delicately. His hand fastened on the looseness of fur behind the neck, lifted quickly, to the mouth of the sack, the sudden feet clamping at the sack, and the head was in, shoved the body. Writhing motion, fierce "meow" of sound. He lifted the bag, keeping his eye on the way the burlap hunched as the cat moved, the way the claws appeared thinly and whitely like slivers, puncturing the bag, the powerful wrestle in there.

At the horse tank he lowered it, took a board and forced it down, a sudden violence of motion as the water penetrated, shrill sound as the woman made, making his neck chill, the fastenings of the claws higher and higher almost to where his left hand gripped the opening of the sack. He looked behind him, around him, never certain of aloneness with three brothers. Only the somnolent yard, the heat, the burned-lemon sun. Long, long he waited. Lifted the heavy bag, dropped it out in the dust. Eyes open as if the dying had come with an immense and terrible surprise, soggy fur, the sudden awareness of how small and thin the creature was, ribs showing racked like toothpick, pinch of tail. He hung the sack in a slat of corncrib to dry, wanted no question from the distrustful brothers or father.

The cat he took by the tail, and the wire, and he went out, across the road, up the path the cows took, up the long hill.

The wild sweet clover, too old to cut, had turned ratty and clumped.

He waited. Squatted in the heat, chewing foxtail stems, waited.

Saw her go finally, past the thukking tractor. The car came and took her away. He waited, the slow Nystrom boy turning the tractor, pausing for water from a jar he had brought, finally going then too.

The boy went at a trot, with a heavy breath in his chest, a lunging dedication to his run as if it must be done at the instant, now and no later. He went up to the one-step porch and turned the knob and went in as if he had done it a thousand times, as if he knew the location of each part and piece of the house from a thousand visitations.

Above the cold stove, by the one side window he suspended the damp dead cat, looped the wire around its neck, hung it from a calendar nail on the wall, feeling the muscles jerk in his slender forearms, glad, God how glad to be freed of this, to have brought it home to her. He watched it sway from its anchor, the electric fur prickled out as if it were alive and fearsomely angry. Looking at it gave him a nervousness, a running of his nose so that he had to rub his sleeve across it. He went out.

Camped behind the chicken coop, he paused, threw desultory clods at the hen dusting itself, went up after a while and sat down along the fence dividing the pasture and the sweet clover patch. In the later afternoon the quality of the heat changed a little, he could feel it, crazy charge that made him want to move his elbows and knees. The cows herded up beneath the thick locust trees in the hollow, the tails lashing at the flies. To the southwest the gray cloud crouched upon the long horizon. Touches of wind came. Whirlwinds funneled, whiskering the fields.

Chill touched his arms. There would be rain, lightning, and hail. A cow bellowed against the flies or its own bones, he did not know.

The fat cloud glowered, puffed, overrode the sun. Far off he could see the thin veins of lightning. Here in stillness, in the oppressive heat he waited. He saw her come, up from the road, running almost, dark-clothed, angular, spider-leg of woman, the storm seemingly at her elbow, the hard gusts of dust snapping around her. He could feel the dust where he squatted.

She went in, hurried, the door open, blowing shut with an astonishing crack. And then he heard one scream, first scream of a woman he'd ever heard, something about it that froze his arteries, and he scrambled backward, turned about in expectation of something terrible all around him, always at his back, and turned and turned again, hearing that terrible echo in his skull, ran sobbing and laughing down to the cattle, the wind and the dust upon him, the first drops of rain thudding. The gray-green vaguely translucent cloud, like looking into the core of an enormity, of the universe, wavered above the hill. There would be hail.

"Come on, cows, come on," he said, shouted finally, propelling them homeward, prodding them. They ran. He ran after, slipping in the mud, glad when the thunder erupted, the hail ripped the trees, drowning the awful sound of screams he yet heard in his hot brain, hearing himself whimper and when he heard that, hearing his own giddy laughter too. She had screamed, screamed terribly, really scared her. He had to laugh.

———◦◄█►◦———

The heated summer passed; dry September came. They went to school again; walked a mile and a quarter to catch the bus. In the evening he got the cows furtively, quickly, with no open look beyond the fence, all was a terrible silence within him. Corner-eyed he glanced, pretended not to see, the blackened shacks, the free door on the cob shed, the gathered dust of road, of field.

"Dry year," old Nystrom said, that big head almost ready to lop from those huge shoulders. "Not much corn this year."

"No," the father said. Not much corn any year where he farmed.

"Guess I'll do the Widow's patch first. Try out the picker over there." Guff of laughter.

"Ain't seen her," the father said. "Lile said she ain't been down to go to Martinsburg at all."

"Oh, she does that sometimes. Gone for a year or more one time, I remember."

"I'm glad she goes away. Gives me the creeps," the mother said.

"No trouble I wonder?" the father said.

"Naw. Not with her," old Nystrom said. "I sent Hank to knock on her door one time. Ask her about picking corn. No answer."

The big-eared young man bent forward eagerly. "Man, I didn't want to do it, afraid she'd jump out at me. But I knocked all right. Guess she went away."

"Ya, she does that," old Nystrom said.

"Good. Brr," the mother said, shaking her thick body. "Gave me the creeps whenever I saw her."

"I'll go down and take a look myself before picking starts," old Nystrom said.

On a stark October afternoon the boy went that way, after school, darted through the dry old sweet clover, the seed heads shattering the little seeds over that dry ground, saw the little lane grown with the tough foxtail, and the ditch run with weeds.

A wind had turned from the north. He shivered. The cob house door banged. There was no chicken, no hen in the coop, dust gathered there in corners. He waited and dawdled around the blackened door, touched with his toe the slivered and weathered step. No sound at all but the suck of wind, scurry of weed and dust.

He rapped upon the door, twice, and jumped back. No sound. If she would answer he would say (heard the words screeching to his ears) he would say, "The Nystroms want to see you." Prepared it. No reply.

Behind him the scurfy field. The blue-white October sun, settling westward. He thought of knocking again, but backed away and went to the one side window.

In the shadows he saw dimly the whitely tufted skeleton of cat, hanging turning ever so slowly in the wind from the shattered window, and there the black clump of skirt huddled, folded by the stove, the one arm draped clutching still the handle of the oven, and the bunch of hair, the socketless eyes, and the face, the teeth, the drawn neck mummified almost, yellow-white, as if screaming yet in that last terrible agony he had heard, the face staring at him, in this total terror, and he heard again, plunging like a blade into his skull, that scream, piercing, shrill. He turned, feeling wet on his face, blubbering, turned and ran blindly, ran with all his might, howling himself, ran and ran, came to the deceptive weed-overgrown ditch, leapt . . .

———————◆◁▷◆◆————————

It was just before noon the next day they found him, burrowed into the ditch at the side of the lane where it made its right angle leading down to the road, his head twisted to one side, the neck broken when he had tried to jump and misjudged and hit the weeded side of the ditch.

His mother set up a howl. All morning she had swung between frenzy and impatience, had said, "Where did he go? Wait till I catch him." Changing to worry.

Now she howled. "He looks like he's asleep. My baby." His neck twisted over, his head resting lightly on his shoulder, his eyes closed almost peacefully, and on his tongue and lower lip a little crumble of dirt, taken as if in ceremony. As if he would awaken and swallow it now.

They carried him, dead and draped, behind them the fire of the buildings that the furious Nystrom had set.

"Poor kid," old Nystrom said. "We shouldn't have talked about her. He was just a curious kid, came up to see for himself what we were talking about, and what he saw was enough to scare anybody, scared me half to death when I saw her in there. Ran away, killed himself like that. She killed him."

"Did you see the cat?" the oldest brother asked. "What was the cat there for?"

"You know her. She was up to something. Like everybody said. No doubt of that. Died herself. Best to burn it all, get clear of it. My fault. I shouldn't have talked about it. Impressionable kid. My fault."

They moved away then, one carrying the peaceful boy, the dirt still on his tongue. They trailed down from the puffing fire, the somber black figures an intrusion on that hard landscape, like a line of stone on that unforgiving horizon.

The Snake

I was thinking of the heat and of water that morning when I was plowing the stubble field far across the hill from the farm buildings. It had grown hot early that day, and I hoped that the boy, my brother's son, would soon come across the broad black area of plowed ground, carrying the jar of cool water. The boy usually was sent out at about that time with the water, and he always dragged an old snow-fence lath or a stick along, to play with. He pretended that the lath was a tractor and he would drag it through the dirt and make buzzing, tractor sounds with his lips.

I almost ran over the snake before I could stop the tractor in time. I had turned at the corner of the field and I had to look back to raise the plow and then to drop it again into the earth, and I was thinking of the boy and the water anyway, and when I looked again down the furrow, the snake was there. It lay half in the furrow and half out, and the front wheels had rolled nearly up to it when I put in the clutch. The tractor was heavily loaded with the weight of the plow turning the earth, and the tractor stopped instantly.

The snake slid slowly and with great care from the new ridge the plow had made, into the furrow and did not go any further. I had never liked snakes much, I still had that kind of quick panic that I'd had as a child whenever I saw one, but this snake was clean and bright and very beautiful. He was multi-colored and graceful and he lay in the furrow and moved his arched and tapered head only so slightly. Go out of the furrow, snake, I said, but he did not move at all. I pulled the throttle of the tractor in and out, hoping to frighten him with the noise, but the snake only flicked its black, forked tongue and faced the huge tractor wheel, without fright or concern.

I let the engine idle then, and I got down and went around the wheel and stood beside it. My movement did frighten the snake and it raised its head and trailed delicately a couple of feet and stopped again, and its tongue was working very rapidly. I followed it, looking at the brilliant colors on its tubular back, the colors clear and sharp and perfect, in orange and green and brown diamonds the size of a baby's fist down its back, and the diamonds were set one within the other and interlaced with glistening jet-black. The colors were astonishing, clear and bright, and it was as if the body held a fire of its own, and the colors came through that transparent flesh and skin, vivid and alive and warm. The eyes were clear and black and the slender body was arched slightly. His flat and gracefully tapered head lifted as I looked at him and the black tongue slipped in and out of that solemn mouth.

You beauty, I said, I couldn't kill you. You are much too beautiful. I had killed snakes before, when I was younger, but there had been no animal like this one, and I knew it was unthinkable that an animal such as that should die. I picked him up, and the length of him arched very carefully and gracefully and only a little wildly, and I could feel the coolness of that radiant, fire-colored body, like splendid ice, and I knew that he had eaten only recently because there were two whole and solid little lumps in the fore-part of him, like field mice swallowed whole might make.

The body caressed through my hands like cool satin, and my hands, usually tanned and dark, were pale beside it, and I asked it where the fire colors could come from the coolness of that body. I lowered him so he would not fall and his body slid out onto the cool, newly plowed earth, from between my pale hands. The snake worked away very slowly and delicately and with a gorgeous kind of dignity and beauty, and he carried his head a little above the rolled clods. The sharp, burning colors of his body stood brilliant and plain against the black soil, like a target.

I felt good and satisfied, looking at the snake. It shone in its bright diamond color against the sun-burned stubble and the crumbled black clods of soil and against the paleness of myself. The color and beauty of it were strange and wonderful and somehow alien, too, in that dry and dusty and uncolored field.

I got on the tractor again and I had to watch the plow closely because the field was drawn across the long hillside and even in that good soil there was a danger of rocks. I had my back to the corner of the triangular field that pointed towards the house. The earth was a little heavy and I had to stop once and clean the plowshares because they were not scouring properly, and I did not look back towards the place until I had turned the corner and was plowing across the upper line of the large field, a long way from where I had stopped because of the snake.

I saw it all at a glance. The boy was there at the lower corner of the field, and he was in the plowed earth, stamping with ferocity and a kind of frenzied impatience. Even at that distance, with no sound but the sound of the tractor, I could tell the fierce mark of brutality on the boy. I could see the hunched-up shoulders, the savage determination, the dance of his feet as he ground the snake with his heels, and the pirouette of his arms as he whipped at it with the stick.

Stop it, I shouted, but the lumbering and mighty tractor roared on, above anything I could say. I stopped the tractor and I shouted down to the boy, and I knew he could hear me, for the morning was clear and still, but he did not even hesitate in that brutal, murdering dance. It was no use. I felt myself tremble, thinking of the diamond light of that beauty I had held a few moments before, and I wanted to run down there and halt, if I could, that frenetic pirouette, catch the boy in the moment of his savagery, and save a glimmer, a remnant, of that which I remembered, but I knew it was already too late. I drove the tractor on, not looking down there; I was afraid to look for fear the evil might still be going on. My head began to ache, and the fumes of the tractor began to bother my eyes, and I hated the job suddenly, and I thought, there are only moments when one sees beautiful things, and these are soon crushed, or they vanish. I felt the anger mount within me.

The boy waited at the corner, with the jar of water held up to me in his hands, and the water had grown bubbly in the heat of the morning. I knew the boy well. He was eleven and we had done many things together. He was a beautiful boy, really, with finely spun blonde hair and a smooth and still effeminate face, and his eyelashes were long and dark and brush-like, and his eyes were blue. He waited there and he smiled as the tractor came up, as he would smile on any other day. He was my nephew, my brother's son, handsome and warm and newly scrubbed, with happiness upon his face and his face resembled my brother's and mine as well.

I saw then, too, the stake driven straight and hard into the plowed soil, through something there where I had been not long before.

I stopped the tractor and climbed down and the boy came eagerly up to me. "Can I ride around with you?" he asked, as he often did, and I had as often let him be on the tractor beside me. I looked closely at his eyes, and he was already innocent; the killing was already forgotten in that clear mind of his.

"No, you cannot," I said, pushing aside the water jar he offered to me. I pointed to the splintered, upright stake. "Did you do that?" I asked.

"Yes," he said, eagerly, beginning a kind of dance of excitement. "I killed a snake; it was a big one." He tried to take my hand to show me.

"Why did you kill it?"

"Snakes are ugly and bad."

"This snake was very beautiful. Didn't you see how beautiful it was?"

"Snakes are ugly," he said again.

"You saw the colors of it, didn't you? Have you ever seen anything like it around here?"

"Snakes are ugly and bad, and it might have bitten somebody, and they would have died."

"You know there are no poisonous snakes in this area. This snake could not harm anything."

"They eat chickens sometimes," the boy said. "They are ugly and they eat chickens and I hate snakes."

"You are talking foolishly," I said. "You killed it because you wanted to kill it, for no other reason."

"They're ugly and I hate them," the boy insisted. "Nobody likes snakes."

"It was beautiful," I said, half to myself.

The boy skipped along beside me, and he was contented with what he had done.

The fire of the colors was gone; there was a contorted ugliness now; the colors of its back were dull and gray-looking, torn and smashed in, and dirty from the boy's shoes. The beautifully tapered head, so delicate and so cool, had been flattened as if in a vise, and the forked tongue splayed out of the twisted, torn mouth. The snake was hideous, and I remembered, even then, the cool, bright fire of it only a little while before, and I thought perhaps the boy had always seen it dead and hideous like that, and had not even stopped to see the beauty of it in its life.

I wrenched the stake out, that the boy had driven through it in the thickest part of its body, between the colored diamond crystals. I touched it and the coolness, the ice-feeling, was gone, and even then it moved a little, perhaps a tiny spasm of the dead muscles, and I hoped that it was truly dead, so that I would not have to kill it. And then it moved a little more, and I knew the snake was dying, and I would have to kill it there. The boy stood off a few feet and he had the stake again and he was racing innocently in circles, making the buzzing tractor sound with his lips.

I'm sorry, I thought to the snake, for you were beautiful. I took the broken length of it around the tractor and I took one of the wrenches from the tool-kit and I struck its head, not looking at it, to kill it at last, for it could never live.

The boy came around behind me, dragging the stake. "It's a big snake, isn't it?" he said. "I'm going to tell everybody how big a snake I killed."

"Don't you see what you have done?" I said. "Don't you see the difference now?"

"It's an ugly, terrible snake," he said. He came up and was going to push at it with his heavy shoes. I could see the happiness in the boy's eyes, the gleeful brutality.

"Don't," I said. I could have slapped the boy. He looked up at me, puzzled, and he swayed his head from side to side. I thought, you little brute, you nasty, selfish, little beast, with brutality already developed within that brain and in those eyes. I wanted to slap his face, to wipe forever the insolence and brutal glee from his mouth, and I decided then, very suddenly, what I would do.

I drew the snake up and I saw the blue eyes of the boy open wide and change and fright, and I stepped towards him as he cringed back, and I shouted, "It's alive, it's alive!" and I looped the tube of the snake's body around the boy's neck.

The boy shrieked and turned in his terror and ran, and I followed a few steps, shouting after him, "It's alive, it's alive, alive!"

The boy gasped and cried out in his terror and he fled towards the distant house, stumbling and falling and rising to run again, and the dead snake hung on him, looped around his neck, and the boy tore at it, but it would not fall off.

The little brute, I thought, the little cruel brute, to hurt and seek to kill something so beautiful and clean, and I couldn't help smiling and feeling satisfied because the boy, too, had suffered a little for his savageness, and I felt my mouth trying to smile about it. And I stopped suddenly and I said, oh God, with the fierce smile of brutality frightening my face, and I thought, oh God, oh God. I climbed quickly onto the tractor and I started it and pulled the throttle open to drown the echoes of the boy shrieking down there in the long valley. I was trembling and I could not steer the tractor well, and I saw that my hands were suffused and flushed, red with a hot blood color.

Lightning Source UK Ltd.
Milton Keynes UK
UKHW012024150722
405892UK00010B/283